Printed by

Sully and Ford,

Plough Court,

Fetter Lane,

London.

THE BRAND

OF THE

BLACK STAR.

By E. H. BURRAGE.

SPLENDIDLY ILLUSTRATED.

THE BRAND
OF THE
BLACK STAR.

—

CHAPTER I.

THE ILL-FATED SUNFLOWER.

WHEN the good ship Sunflower sailed from Liverpool she bore away with her some light-hearted, hopeful people, going abroad to seek the good fortune that was denied to them at home. The usual dreams were theirs—of a few years' sojourn abroad, a fortune made, and a return to the Old Country to enjoy it.

Alas! for the dreams of the majority.

The Sunflower was bound for the Cape, but when she was hundreds of miles short of her destination she encountered a cyclone that drove her out of her course, reduced her to a complete wreck, and finally left her helpless and adrift.

It was a gloomy time for all—the captain silent and troubled, the officers and crew dejected, the passengers in doubt and terror as to what might be in store for them.

Happily, there were few women on board. The emigrants for the most part were strong men, ready and able to rough it in a new land. Among them were James Standish and Herbert, his son.

Standish was a man of great muscular power, and one might have taken him for a blacksmith, but for his manner, which was that of an educated man.

His son Herbert was sixteen years of age, but looked older, and was modelled in the same fashion as his father, broad-shouldered and upright as a dart, with a handsome, restful face, such as would be composed even in moments of great excitement. The eyes of both were grey, and sparkling with intelligence.

They sailed as third-class passengers, and great curiosity as to who they were was expressed by their fellow-passengers among themselves.

But as neither offered any information, nobody cared to ask a question on the subject.

Neither father nor son looked as if they would tolerate anything in the way of impertinence.

But they were popular among the passengers because they were genial and unaffected, and in the heart of one man they excited a feeling amounting to devotion.

This was one Samuel Gorgon, who had been all sorts of things at home, and failed in everything, and was now going abroad to try his luck.

Gorgon had a comical face that would have made his fortune on the stage, and if he had only spoken on the boards in his natural manner he would have been accepted as the leading comedian of the day.

But, strange to say, he had never thought of the stage, and had gone in for all sorts of serious things to get a living, and naturally failed in all.

These three were standing together in the bows of the Sunflower, looking ahead at what seemed to be a cloud in the horizon, but which the sailors declared to be land.

Close behind them was Nero, a huge mastiff dog belonging to the captain.

It had attached itself to Herbert, and soon apparently had a greater affection for him than its original master.

"Well, any land will be welcome," said James Standish, "after drifting helplessly about the sea."

"The sailors say it is not inhabited, sir," said Sam Gorgon.

Sam was invariably polite, and the "sir" was a relic of his old business days.

"As far as they know," said Herbert, "the coast is a mountainous one."

"You can't tell," said his father.   "The mountains may be many miles inland."

Several other passengers then drew up behind them, and the conversation became general.

That the Sunflower was drifting towards the coast was certain, and the great question was what sort of coast would they find it to be.

If a rocky one, with dangerous reefs and the attendant breakers, the prospect was a poor one, but if there was a sandy beach landing would be an easy matter.

How anxiously they watched for indications of the nature of the coast.

A strong wind was blowing towards the land, and as it steadily increased there was a prospect of its blowing a gale before sunset.

And they could only drift; for the Sunflower was a mere log upon the sea.

Presently the captain, watching through his glass, detected a white line all along the horizon.

A pallor overspread his face, not so much on his own account as for the helpless beings in his charge.

There were three hundred on board, and, in case of wreck, how many could hope to reach the shore alive?

The captain gave orders quietly for such means of saving life as they had on board to be got ready.

Boats there were none.

They had all been swept away by the terrible cyclone.

Ere long the passengers saw the white line, and some said "it was the white cliffs of the coast such as they had left behind them at home;" but the silence of the sailors showed they had other thoughts concerning the whitening horizon.

And the wind, increasing, blew the Sunflower landward at almost ordinary sailing pace.

The tide, too, was in the favour of the powers of destruction.

A big swell was on, but the sea was smooth-topped around the vessel, save for an occasional "curler."

Gradually the coast drew near, and the thunderous sounds of breakers reached their ears like the humming of bees.

It increased in strength, and a plain view of the waves beating on the rocks was obtained.

We need not dwell upon the incidents of the next half-hour.

Any further concealment of the perils of their position would have been foolish and unkind.

The captain called all on board together, and in a few brief words explained the prospect before them.

"We must trust in Providence," he said, "and behave like men."

To the few women on board were given the life-belts, and the men were told to avail themselves of anything they could find.

Hen-coops, planks, chairs, and a score other things were brought into requisition.

Sam Gorgon bound himself to an empty barrel, but the Standishes, father and son, imitated the sailors, who did no more than kick off their shoes and remove their extra upper clothing.

A short service was held, the captain reading a simple prayer for those in peril at sea.

Then a general hand-shaking took place, but little was said.

The women wept quietly and the men were pale, but there was no unworthy panic.

And now the breakers were very near, and the crashing and lashing of the angry waters drowned all other sounds.

The Sunflower went to her doom, as it seemed to Herbert Standish, with leaps and bounds.

Crash !

The good ship was on a rock, and the work of destruction had begun.

King Death hovered triumphantly aloft, and as the ship heeled over half the passengers rolled into the foaming sea.

Husbands and wives were parted, never to meet again.   It was impossible for one to give any help to them.

Friend saw friend go down into the sea and disappear.

A hand or an arm would perchance rise here and there out of the foam, but only to disappear again.   An awful spectacle for those still clinging to the wreck.

Herbert and his father clung to the ratline stanchions on the upper side of the doomed vessel, their arms linked together, both composed and ready for the worst.

Sam Gorgon and his barrel had disappeared; but Nero, the dog, remained close to Herbert, holding on to the side of the vessel with his paws.

Suddenly Herbert saw the deck open right across, just as one would part a stick of ginger-bread, the noise of the breaking up being very faintly heard above the roar of the breakers.

Herbert looked up at his father and smiled, and the father, bending down, kissed him on the forehead.

That, in case of all being lost, was their last adieu.

Three seconds sufficed to open the Sunflower to her keel, and then each portion of her rolled different ways, one on either side of the line of rocks upon which she had struck, and became engulphed.

Brief the battle for life among the majority.

A number of black specks were seen among the foam, rapidly disappearing one by one.

A few cries, heartrending and despairing, were heard, and that was all.

A few atoms of humanity were carried shorewards, fiercely battling for existence.

Over a second line of breakers they went, their numbers diminishing on the other side.

Only the strongest or those especially favoured by Providence could hope to live.

The shore itself was nothing but coarse shingle and shattered rocks—a hard resting-place for a sufferer to be cast upon.

It seemed impossible to be cast upon it and live.

And yet some survived, being cast bleeding, exhausted, and gasping upon the uncharitable stones.

But they *lived*, and out of their marvellous escape from Death comes our tale.

CHAPTER II.

THE CASTAWAYS.

" HERBERT !"

The boy heard the voice and awoke as from a long and weary sleep.

He was lying on the shingle, and his father,

heedless of an ugly cut upon his own forehead, was bending over him.

"What is the matter, pater?" Herbert asked.

And then his memory brought back events to him.

"Are we saved?" he exclaimed. "I thought all were lost."

"There are three of us here, if no more," his father replied.

He pointed to the left, where Nero, the dog, lay stretched upon the shingle in a state of great exhaustion, but with his eyes on Herbert—speaking eyes, that said, "I'm glad *you* are here, anyway."

Herbert felt as if he had been beaten all over with heavy sticks, but he managed to rise, and, with his father, look about him.

Up and down the shore were signs of the wreck —portions of the vessel, large bales and packages, part of the cargo, and here and there a still form of man or woman.

"Some may yet live," said James Standish. "Rest here, while I see if I can help them."

"I can come too," said Herbert.

His example stimulated the dog. Nero got upon his feet, and, having been patted by Herbert, hobbled after them in a rheumaticky way.

The first still form they came to was that of the captain. He was dead, and so on for half a dozen others, and then they came to a fine man whom they had known on board the Sunflower as Richard Warden.

He was a quiet, well-spoken man, and, like the Standishes, had little to say about his past.

They found him lying beside a rock, staring at the sky in a dazed manner, and at first could not render him sensible of where he was.

But he, like the Standishes, soon got the better

of his recent struggle for life, and having no bones broken, got upon his feet.

And that was all the signs of life that could be found.

Not one-sixth of the hapless passengers and crew of the Sunflower had come ashore, and of that portion these three and the dog seemed to be the sole survivors.

They rested together for awhile, talking over their merciful escape, and then sought some food, of which there was plenty cast ashore.

Barrels of pickled pork, biscuit, flour, tobacco, and packages of other things were scattered about up and down the coast.

They broke open a barrel of biscuit with big stones, and satisfied their modest wants for a time, and then surveyed the land behind them.

The mountains seen from the sea were many miles inland, and the intervening country was of a very promising nature.

There was wood and water, and possibly fruit, and close to the sea were several small hills, from any of which they could command a view of a wide stretch of water.

What chance they had of being rescued none could tell; they could only guess at it, and the guess of one and all was not in the hopeful direction.

But they did not despair.

The amount of useful material cast ashore from the wreck was immense.

They found biscuits, flour, pickled and preserved meats, a considerable amount of groceries, and many other things.

Then again, neither portions of the wreck were in deep water, and when the tide was out they were able to reach them.

From these they got arms and ammunition and

the chests of the seamen and passengers. There could be no sin in taking the things of the dead, so they broke open the chests, and, having selected what was useful, stored them away on shore.

Suits of clothes and all sorts of apparatus for a digger's life fell into their hands.

Needles, thread, knives, forks, metal plates, carpenters' tools, picks, spades, and so on.

They had enough to utilise twenty men as assistants.

To Herbert it was the dawn of a new life. He could but be sorry for the dead, but he could not help rejoicing in the present.

" We are here," he said, " *alone*—three Robinson Crusoes."

And so it seemed, for they could find no trace of living beings—present or past.

Richard Warden had had some experience of a settler's life, and was, in addition, a very handy fellow with the chisel, hammer, and saw.

Having chosen a spot about a mile inland, where there were both wood and water, he marked out two spots for the erection of huts, and proceeded to prepare the timber, while Herbert and his father brought up the spoils of the wreck.

It is almost needless to say that they showed respect for their late companions by burying all the dead that came ashore.

Their numbers were few, not more than a score at the outside ; the rest had vanished.

Not even when the tide was out were traces found of them.

This at first appeared strange, but with each tide a great shifting of sand between the rocks was observable, so they presumed that the sea had played the part of sexton, and regretted them as lost.

Within a week they became reconciled to their unenviable lot and settled down to make the best of things.

At first they kept a constant look-out for a possibly passing vessel, but the semi-circular line of water was not broken by a sail, and they soon relaxed their vigilance.

"We've got to live here," said Herbert, "for a time at least."

Game of all sorts abounded in the district. Deer came at eve to the stream hard by to drink, and one well-directed shot supplied the larder with meat for many days.

"It isn't exactly what we looked for, Herbert," said his father; "but it will do."

"Do !" exclaimed Herbert, with the enthusiasm of youth; "I should think it would. I call it a glorious life."

"If it lasts," thought his father. "But if I or Warden should die—or perchance both—what will become of you, my son ?"

Warden was a splendid companion. He was brave, hopeful, cheery, and useful.

The log huts he designed were, in their way, models. They had all sorts of rugged comforts which half the pioneers of civilisation have not known.

The huts were strongly built, warm, and dry, and the climate was perfect.

Three weeks were occupied in building and fitting them up, and the time passed quickly.

No rain marred their labours. The sky at day was a cloudless blue.

At night innumerable stars studded the heavens, and a cool, gentle breeze mollified a portion of the heat.

"Surely," said James Standish, "we have fallen upon the original Paradise !"

As for Nero, the dog, he was as happy as a dog could be.

Like the men, he recovered his health and strength, and passed his time in congenial society.

He stopped at night with the Standishes. Richard Warden slept in his own hut.

"I have always longed for a house of my own, and never got one until now," he said a dozen times; "don't think I am selfish if I enjoy it."

When all had been done that was needed for their domestic comfort the two took to exploring the country together, going out early in the morning, carrying their rations for the day, and returning at eve, heartily weary, to sleep away the dark hours in perfect rest.

This sort of life they led for weeks, until one night came when Herbert was suddenly awakened in the middle of the night by the barking of Nero.

James Standish was still soundly sleeping, and the dog, at the bidding of his young master, ceased to bark.

But he went up to the door, sniffing and growling there for awhile.

"Some animal prowling around," thought Herbert.

He was too tired to rise for a time, but at last, as Nero continued his uneasy movements at the door, he got up to take a peep at things outside.

Opening the door half way, and keeping the dog back with a movement of his arm, he peered out.

The stars were shining brightly, and he could see with tolerable distinctness for some distance around.

Nothing living, man or beast, was in sight.

"It is nothing," said Herbert, and returned to his couch, made of bedding taken from the Sunflower.

Nero came over to his side and lay down, as if he, too, was satisfied.

So Herbert, reassured, sought sleep again, and was soon once more in the land of forgetfulness.

CHAPTER III.

THE BRAND OF THE BLACK STAR.

WITH the return of the day Herbert had cause for further uneasiness.

Awakening before his father, he went out with Nero, and the dog at once began to sniff around the hut as if expecting to see some foe not far away.

But after a while the dog ceased these movements, and the two men coming out of their huts simultaneously, morning greetings were exchanged, and a fire lighted as a preliminary to breakfast.

"Shall I say anything or not?" Herbert thought.

And after some reflection he elected to keep his own counsel.

"It *must* have been some animal prowling around the light."

That day a journey in the direction of the mountains had been arranged for, with a view to properly estimate their distance and decide whether they should make an attempt to reach them.

The nature of the land beyond might be favourable to their natural desire to return to civilisation.

At the same time, they were not in a hurry to abandon the comforts of their present position, and risk starvation in a sterile land.

About eight miles away there was a hill of some magnitude—at home we should call it a small mountain—and from the summit of this they hoped to get a view of the far-off mountains which would enable them to judge of the country around.

As they would, in taking a direct line, have to traverse a wood which they suspected to be luxuriantly dense, they, by the advice of Richard Warden, armed themselves with axes to cut through the expected impediments of vines and other undergrowth.

Everything around them grew with surpassing luxuriance, and in the wood there could be no exception to the rule.

Already they had discovered such displays of wild fruit and flowers as they had not even dreamt of or found any parallel to, even in the books of travels.

The direction they took that morning was a new one to the adventurers.

It was a day full of delights to a lover of nature.

They forced their way through the wood, which proved to be of moderate extent, leaving a track to guide them home, reached the summit of the hill, and surveyed the mountains ahead.

Apparently they were barren and destitute of even minor vegetation, and chilled by the prospect they set out for home.

"We are in a paradise," said James Standish, "shut out from the world by desolate mountains. They form a huge semi-circle around us."

Somehow, the discovery had a depressing effect upon all there. Their charming home assumed the nature of a prison, and half its charm was frittered away.

Their homeward journey was more silent than usual, and as they drew near the huts Nero again began to show signs of restlessness.

But the dog only sniffed the air suspiciously,

trotting onward without leaving the side of Herbert.

At length they came in sight of their "home," and Richard Warden's hut was the first reached.

There a tremendous surprise—it might be called a shock—awaited them.

Coarsely painted on the door was a big black star !

It had been drawn either hurriedly or by a hand possessing only the elementary knowledge of drawing ; but the fact of its being there was sufficient.

For fully half a moment they all stood still, silently staring at the strange and—as they could not help feeling—ominous sign.

"What does it mean ?" exclaimed Richard Warden at last.

"Heaven and he who did it only knows," replied James Standish, between his set teeth.

They turned to look at the hut occupied by Herbert and his father, but there was no similar sign upon it.

Thither they went first, and opened the door, fully expecting some savage foe to leap out upon them.

But nobody was there.

Nothing had been disturbed.

Somewhat reassured, they went to Richard Warden's hut, and found the interior free from spoliation.

As far as they could see there were no signs of intrusion.

Nor were there any traces of footsteps outside— nothing but that dismal black star to tell them that a stranger had been there.

"I've got it," said Richard Warden, suddenly ; "this is some joke."

"And who may the jester be ?" asked Herbert.

"Some of our old friends who have escaped the wreck. It could easily be done—a brush, a tin of ship's tar, and—"

"This is no ship's tar," interposed James Standish, "nor any class of paint that I am acquainted with. No, Warden, your theory will not do. We must look further and deeper for the solution of the mystery. In any case you sleep no more alone."

"Pooh! nonsense," exclaimed Warden. "I'm not afraid of it. I am as certain as I can be that it is only a joke."

"But where is the fun of it?"

"Well, that is for the joker to explain. He will be looking around here directly, with a grin upon his face."

His did his best to make light of it, and he insisted on occupying his hut at night, as he had hitherto done.

"A daub of paint doesn't scare me out of *my* house," he said, "and I can barricade the door if I like. You may reckon nobody can get in without there being a bit of a shindy first."

It was in vain to argue with him; he only laughed, and said he would be ready for the „joker," and "get the grin on the other side."

All he would do was to consent to their supping together, as usual, in the open air.

They were all pretty well tired out, and when the meal was over Richard Warden lighted his pipe and got upon his feet.

"Good-night, comrades," he said. "If I should oversleep myself in the morning you can knock me up. I've got a notion of making a trap for the star-painting gentleman—an improvement on the old bear-trap. We will set it to-morrow."

He went, closing the door behind him, and they waited for awhile, expecting to hear him barricade himself in.

Coarsely painted on the door was a big black star.

But there was no indication that he intended to do so, and with something like a frown on his face James Standish signed to Herbert to go in.

" We have the dog," he said, " but he has nothing.   Herbert, I am *sure* this is no jest."

They went to rest, and soon slept, but not for long.   Within an hour both father and son were awakened by the loud barking of Nero, who was trying to tear his way through the door.

With all speed they struck a light and aroused themselves.   Then they opened the door and looked out.

Then a terrible spectacle met their view.
Richard Warden's hut was on fire!

CHAPTER IV.

WHO FIRED THE HUT?—A MISSING FRIEND— TRACES OF THE FOE.

IT was the roof of the hut that was on fire near the summit of its gentle slope, and the first thought of father and son was to give the alarm to Richard Warden.

Herbert, the swiftest of foot, reached the door first, and finding it ajar he kicked it open and called on Warden to come out.

But there was no answer from within, nor was anybody in sight.

The fire, having burned a hole in the roof, cast a lurid glow around the interior of the building, exhibiting it in its usual state.

No signs of disorder met the eye, and not the least indication of a struggle.

But Richard Warden was gone.

Nero went into the hut and sniffed around, while Herbert and his father held a hurried consultation.

" Perhaps he has only gone out for awhile,"

said James Standish, "and the fire may be an accidental one.   We had better try to save some of his things."

The hut they could not save, for, although they had water handy and buckets from the ship, the former only trickled slowly from a spring and could be of no service.

Ere two buckets could be filled the hut would be burned to the ground.

So they contented themselves with saving what they could from the fire.

Among the multifarious articles brought in from the wreck and apportioned to Richard Warden were two barrels of powder, and these were first removed, not without considerable peril, for the flakes of fire fell fast around Herbert and his father.

They worked hard, and in a few minutes had got the most valuable portion of the portable things outside.

Then they were obliged to desist from working, for the roof was well alight and every moment threatened to collapse and fall.

This, indeed, did happen a few moments later, and for a brief space of time it seemed as if the fire was extinguished.

But it speedily burst out again, and a column of fire rose up straight in the still air, making all things around almost as clear to the eye as in the day-time.

There was no more sleep for father and son that night.

Having stored Warden's things in their own hut, they kept watch outside with loaded rifles, trusting mainly to the instinct of Nero to give warning of the approach of a foe.

But the dog lay stretched upon the ground, staring at the fire with blinking eyes, and gave no sign.

The burning hut blazed fiercely, for it had been built of a species of pine, and the turpentine in it was a great assistant to the conflagration.

It also burned long, and fully two hours elapsed ere the fiercer light subsided, and gradually settled down until only a glowing mass of ashes remained.

It still wanted at least another two hours to daylight, and the gloom was doubly deep after the bright light.

But the two watchers kept to their post, occasionally exchanging a few words in whispers.

At last the day returned, and they could look about for some traces of their missing friend.

The hope that he would return, which had earlier been in their hearts, died away.

They could only believe that he was dead.

Two things remained for them to do—to take measures to protect themselves, and if an opportunity offered to avenge his death.

Their first care was to look around the destroyed hut for traces of footsteps ; but the ground was hard and dry, and they found none.

Herbert picked up a piece of metal, but it was of a strange nature to him, and to James Standish also, being neither iron, steel, or brass, nor any substance with which they were acquainted.

This and a small piece of finely-woven grass-matting, about four inches square, was all they could discover.

It was not much, but it seemed to show that Richard Warden was not gone away on his own account.

Somewhere around a foe was concealed.

"There are a thousand hiding-places for them," said James Standish, "but after all they may be few in number, and I will not budge until I know who or what they are."

"No—we will not budge," said Herbert.

They felt the loss of their late companion greatly
—for apart from his being an addition to their
number he had been a cheery and useful companion.   It worried them both, but outwardly
neither exhibited any sign of their feelings.

Their first care was to endeavour to find some
trace of the way the foe had taken; but they failed
to do so.

"It will be useless to attempt to explore the
country," said James Standish.   "We've got to
wait here until they come, and they must not find
us unprepared.

Their next step was to cut down some sapling
trees and put a rough *cheveaux de frise* round the
hut.

The upper parts of it were left jagged, and
being put close together, it was a very awkward
thing for a man to climb over.

One narrow opening was left for them to pass
through.

It was exactly opposite the door, which was
pierced for firing through at a foe.   Only one man
at a time could approach the door.

This work occupied them for three days, and
during that time they were unmolested.

At night they slept in turns, and Nero, night
and day, seemed to be ever on the watch.

They talked of the strange sign they had found
upon the door, "the Black Star," and endeavoured
in every possible way to fathom its meaning, but
they had absolutely nothing to give them a solution
to the mystery.

"We can only *wait*," said James Standish.

The wooden fence around the house being completed they felt more at ease, and the continued
absence of a foe gradually brought back quietude.

Of course things were not the same, for Richard
Warden was not there, and the mystery of his

disappearance remained to harass them ; but men learn to adapt themselves to anything in time, and the two brave settlers soon became again at ease.

A week had elapsed, when one morning they left their hut together, and accompanied by Nero, wended their way in the direction of the sea.

It was their intention to fish from the shore when the tide was in, and Herbert carried the lines over his left shoulder.

In his right hand he carried the ever-ready rifle.

As they emerged from the last bit of wood and stood before the open sea Nero suddenly became alert, looked quickly to the right and left, uttered a deep growl, and then bounded towards the beach.

Herbert's eyes following the dog saw a sleeping figure on the sands.

He was too far off to make out exactly what it was, but it seemed to him as if it was some huge baboon on all fours.

The dog dashed towards the figure.

It rose up, and then it was seen that it was a man.

The cry he uttered faintly reached the ears of the Standishes as they bounded forward with cocked rifles in their hands.

They saw Nero dash up to the stranger, spring upon him, and hurl him over on the shore.

"Hurry up, Herbert," cried James Standish. "I think we have got hold of one who will explain the mystery of the Black Star."

Herbert did not stand in need of any admonition.

With a quickened pulse and feet as fleet as those of the greyhound he was bearing down upon the spot where Nero and the figure were tumbling about the sands.

CHAPTER V.

FRIENDS, NOT FOES—MORE OF THE SAVED— THE FATAL SIGN.

" TAKE the dog off him !" cried James Standish.
" Don't let him worry the man, Herbert."

" All right, pater," sung out Herbert.

As he ran up, he saw that Nero was not exactly worrying the man.

On the contrary, they were rolling about in playful, friendly embrace, and the man was laughing in quite an hysterical manner.

" Good dog !" he was crying ; " good old Nero ! Oh ! what a meeting. Here's a time of real good business ! Good Nero—good old dog !"

There was no mistaking that cheery, unmusical voice, although it was cracked and a little out of tune.

It was Sam Gorgon who was thus hailing the dog as an old friend.

Nero did not spring upon him in anger, but in playfulness, and the meeting was one of old friends, and not of foes.

" Sam," cried Herbert—everybody on board the Sunflower used to call Gorgon by his Christian name—" how came you here ? Off, Nero—be quiet !"

The dog dislodged himself from Sam's embrace, and then, rising up, stared at Herbert with his eyes like two beads just stuck upon his head.

" Don't tell me I am dreaming," cried Sam. " Is it you ?"

" It's me, and nobody else," replied Herbert, with a tinge of hysteria in his own voice. " Get up and shake hands with me."

" Give me a hand," said Sam. " I'm quite limp with astonishment. Why, as I live, here's your father, too ! Business is looking up this morning !"

They got him on his feet and shook hands with him until they were tired, while Nero lay upon the sand lolling his big tongue out, and looking the picture of doggy happiness.

"Tell me," said Sam, "how you came here?"

"First tell us how you escaped?" said Herbert.

"I can't," replied Sam Gorgon. "I don't know how it was done.   All I can tell you is that I came ashore with that barrel, rolling and twisting and turning over and over, swallowing salt water by the bucketful, and gasping like a grampus or a whale, and I was thrown up and left in such a state that I thought I was turned into a jelly-fish."

"And what have you been doing since?" asked James Standish.

"Oh! we've been staring and poking about," replied Gorgon; "living on green leaves and shell-fish."

"We? Who's we?"

"Oh! there are half-a-dozen more. There s Ginger the boatswain, three of the crew, and two of the first-class passengers—twin brothers of the name of Trevelyn, David and John. You can't tell t'other from which, and for a long time neither was certain which had been saved from drowning. It was only when they found that both were alive that either could persuade himself that he was saved."

"And that is all?" said James Standish.

"Oh! no," said Sam Gorgon; "there's another sample of goods—I mean another man saved. You remember a man named Carroll, a moody sort of chap, who was always certain something was going to happen. They used to call him Jonah the Prophet, and it was suggested he should be tossed overboard. Well, he's with us."

"And does he prophesy still?" asked Herbert.

"Oh! yes; he's at it every day. He is sure

something is going to happen. We are all living —if living it can be called—in a cave half-a-mile higher up, near where we landed. We've fancied that we must be somewhere near, close to the wreck ; but until to-day we thought we were on the other side of it. Everybody got into a regular muddle in the sea that day. But, I say, how did you escape ?"

"We will tell you as we go along," said James Standish ; "let us go and see the rest."

"They're mighty thin," said Sam Gregon, with a faint smile ; "you will hardly know 'em ; but you can't expect us to get fat on leaves and shell-fish."

Poor Sam ! He was almost a skeleton himself, and was as much in need of food as anybody.

He was so excited that he would have made a bad listener, and the Standishes made no attempt to tell him the story of their miraculous escape and subsequent adventures.

He led the way along the beach round a point which hid the spot of the wreck from view, and Herbert was beginning to understand how ship-wrecked men cast weak and helpless upon a shore would, under the circumstances, fail to observe the work that was done by his father, himself, and Richard Warden when they cleared the ship.

Nevertheless, some further explanation was necessary to make these matters quite clear, and this was in due time forthcoming, as the reader will see.

In a cave, or, rather, outside it, at that moment, were the others who had been fortunate enough to escape a watery grave.

First of all there was Ginger, the boatswain—a shock-headed, sturdy man, with a face expressive of much dogged determination.

He was sitting on a stone looking seaward, and

close behind him stood two young men as like as two peas.

These were the twin brothers Trevelyn, quietly dressed, and looking like young fellows who could meet the storms of life like brave men.

Hard by was Carroll, the misanthrope, a dark, moody-looking man, engaged in conversation with the three seamen who made up the party.

On the meeting we need not dwell.

It was a joyous one, as it could not help being under the circumstances.

Carroll alone exhibited no pleasing emotion.

"It's all right, I suppose," he said; "but I feel just as if your coming would bring us further trouble."

Then uprose Ginger, the boatswain, to denounce him, which he did in good round terms as a man who grumbled at misfortune and acted "like a lump of lead on the sperrits of the party."

"Well, tell me what hopes we've got of escaping starvation," said Carroll, "and I'll be as cheerful as any of you."

"You need not starve yet," said James Standish, quietly.

And then he told them of the things which had been saved from the wreck—of barrels of biscuits and flour, preserved meat, general provisions, and other things.

Then it came out that but for Ginger, the boatswain, all there might have been present at the clearing out of the wreck.

Insisting upon his nautical knowledge, Ginger declared that the wreck lay in the opposite direction, and it seemed he had brought a vast amount of navigator's lore to bear upon the question.

On the sands with a piece of stick he had drawn charts of winds, tides, and currents, proving to everybody that the wreck *must* be lying north if anywhere, whereas, it so happened that it had been lying south.

Even now he was not quite convinced.

"South it may be," he said, "but north it ought to be. Anyway, my lads, I'll be glad to get another nibble at ship's biscuit, and should there be a weevil in it I'll not be the man to grumble."

Up to the present neither Herbert nor his father had spoken of the mysterious disappearance of Richard Warden.

Men in a half-starved condition, with their nerves unstrung, were not in a condition to listen to a story fraught with the mysterious and the terrible.

By-and-bye, when they had eaten and were stronger, would be time enough for the narration.

The first thing to be done was to guide them to his house in the woods, and this he did with a dim fear that something might have happened to it in his absence.

Nor were his fears without foundation.

The men walked slowly, and the morning was more than half-spent when they came in sight of the hut with its stockade around it.

"Why, you look as if you expected to be besieged," said David Trevelyn, one of the twins.

"It is well to be prepared for all probabilities," said Herbert, who was walking by his side.

Ah! it was well indeed for *him* to be prepared, for the next moment his eye fell upon the star painted on the door of his house in the same crude fashion he had witnessed before.

His father had seen it, too, but they did not so much as exchange a look.

With composed faces they led the way to the door and pushed it open.

Inside there were no signs of a foe.

Nothing had been taken or disturbed.

"I see you've got a sign up," said Ginger, pointing to the star. "It makes a man feel just as if he was going into a comfortable inn."

"The Star of Hope," suggested John Trevelyn.

His voice was so like that of his brother that Herbert looked at David as he answered—

"We do not consider it exactly the Star of Hope, but we will not accept it as a sign of despair. Enter and eat, and after that we will tell you its story."

CHAPTER VI.

WATCH AND WAIT—A DAY OF LANGUOR— FATAL WORK FOLLOWING THE FATAL SIGN.

THEY had all eaten a hearty meal such as half-starved men would partake of, and afterwards James Standish, in a simple, unaffected way, told them the story of the Black Star and Richard Warden's disappearance.

"I presume," he said by way of conclusion, "that I am talking to men who have stout hearts within them. What this sign may mean, or who-ever are the secret foes we may have to contend with, maybe, it would not become us to exhibit any craven fears. We must find out whom we have to fight against and fight them."

"Hear, hear!" cried Ginger, and there was a murmur of approval all round.

It rose to a chorus of jubilation when James Standish went on to explain that he had arms enough to supply them with at least one weapon apiece, and ammunition to last for a pretty long course of casual fighting.

He was at once elected as their chief, with Herbert for his lieutenant.

As all could not sleep in that small hut the work of erecting others was at once begun.

James Standish still kept to his watchword—
"Wait"—and declared that any exploration in
search of the secret foe might only lead them astray.

"Poor Warden was caught napping," he said;
"but it may be otherwise with me. If a hundred
Black Stars were painted on my door I should not
look upon myself as a doomed man."

"Perhaps it may be meant for you soon," said
Carroll, gloomily.

"Oh! you dunderhead," said Sam Gorgon.
"A pretty sort of man of business you would make.
Not that it matters, for Herbert is no more
frightened than his father. How do you know,
Carroll, it isn't meant for *you*? Perhaps they were
advised by their firm, I mean their captain,
that you were coming."

"It is more than likely," said Carroll, with a
despairing look. "I have felt ever since I started
on that ill-fated voyage that I was doomed to die
abroad."

They were angry with him, but they could not
laugh at the man, for really he seemed to be something of a prophet in his way, and the situation
was sufficiently serious not to be made a jest of.

They all examined the star on the door, and
declared it to be done with some sort of paint, the
like of which they had never seen before.

It had fairly soaked into the wood, and to remove
it without destroying the door was impossible.

"Let it remain," said James Standish, "unless
it troubles anyone here more than it does me."

They let it remain, and bold and light-hearted
in their numerality they went to work, cutting
down small timber and building other log huts for
their habitations.

One large one was erected for the use of Ginger
and the seamen, and another for the twin-brothers,
Carroll, and Sam Gorgon.

It was the work of days, and no foe appeared to check them in their labours.

But the star remained on the door.

The paint, instead of fading, grew brighter under the sunlight, and at night it was aglow, as if it was a phosphorescent production.

But it gave out no odour.

This added to the mystery of it, and ere two days had elapsed its mysterious presence began to work upon the superstitious sailors.

"It isn't of the earth," they would whisper to each other. "Mr. Warden has been spirited away."

And what is more their brethren, more enlightened, began to think there was something uncany about it.

What hand painted it?

In that lone land, with no sign of civilisation, and, beyond themselves, no indication of habitation, who was there that could have painted such a crude sign?

"It's like a trade mark," said Sam Gorgon, "and it means serious business."

"We shall see what it means," said James Standish to his son; "let us wait."

They waited and watched, but the hidden enemy did not emerge from his secret place.

In parties of two or three, all well armed, they took it in turns to make a circuit around and never once did they come upon anything which would give them a clue to the enemy.

A theory was started that after all there might be no enemy in the case.

Richard Warden had been known on board the Sunflower as one, who loved a jest. Might he not now be exercising his love of a joke upon his friends?

"He is not such a fool," said Herbert, "and

one simple thing scouts the idea. From whence could he get that curious paint? Last night it was dry. This morning when I touched it with my finger it was wet."

"It can't be explained," said Carroll.

But when a number of men are together they are slow to show craven fear, and in the two Standishes the party had heart-inspiring leaders.

Herbert, though but a youth, bore himself as a man, and would sometimes steal away into the wood alone, armed with nothing but his axe, and then in solitude fell a tree as if in defiance of the hidden enemy.

His father expostulated with him more than once, but he only laughed.

"Do you fear the Brand of the Black Star?" he cried.

"No," replied his father.

"Would you have *me* fear it?'

"No."

"Then do not attempt to hinder me in my movements. Let me come and go as if we were in one of the dear old woods at home."

"Ah! the woods at home," sighed James Standish.

The brothers Trevelyn were excellent fellows— good companions at home, excellent hunters abroad.

They were much attached to Herbert, and often when he was going out with his axe upon his shoulder would ask him if they might accompany him.

But he always said, "No, I prefer being alone."

Although he exhibited only the axe, Herbert had a pair of revolvers concealed and ready for use.

As he worked his eyes were ever on the watch for some creeping foe; he felt assured that to him would come the solution of the mystery of Rich ard Warden's disappearance.

In a little while the whole party began to scatter itself in the morning, some going one way, others another—some to work, some to seek game for food.

At last there came one broiling hot day, with the air so sultry that all said it portended the gathering of a terrible storm.

A lassitude was on all ere they went out to work.

Even Herbert, usually so elastic and buoyant, felt it.

He had marked a tree for cutting down on the previous eve, and towards it he wended his way.

His boots seemed to be shod with lead—the air half stifled him.

Arriving at the spot for his work, he sat down upon the ground to rest.

The heat and closeness of the air almost overcame him.

" I can't work to-day," he said, after a while. " There is thunder in the air. Perhaps something like the monsoon of India I have read about is approaching."

He turned slowly back, walking at a crawl, and pausing now and then with a dreamy lassitude upon him which no effort he could make would shake off.

" It is just as if the air were drugged," he said to himself.

He was some time in reaching the encampment, and it was just visible through the trees when he heard a faint cry ahead.

In a moment he was aroused to action.

Grasping his axe firmly, he ran forward and reached the clearing. It was divided by all save

On the rude flooring was painted the now too ominous star.

one of the brothers Trevelyn, who was standing by the door of Herbert's home.

He looked like a man on whom a heavy blow had fallen, and as Herbert came towards him, he gasped out—

"Come here—quick—the enemy has been to your house."

Fearing some horrible catastrophe, Herbert hurried in and saw the table upset and the place in confusion.

At first he could see no more, a sudden dimness overcame his sight.

Trevelyn—it was David—followed him in, and leaning one hand on the fallen table, cried—

"There ! Do you see it ?"

And Herbert looked with all his eyes.

On the rude flooring was painted the now too ominous star.

"And here !" almost shrieked David.

Now he pointed under the overturned table, and Herbert there beheld the form of a man, whose attitude alone proclaimed that he was dead.

"My *father !*" he cried.

"No," replied David Trevelyn ; " it is Carroll. His prophecy has been fulfilled ; he has died abroad. But your father—"

"What of him ?" asked Herbert, with a sudden stillness upon him.

"He was here a little while ago," replied David. " I saw him enter the house with Carroll, and I went away, only for a few minutes. When I returned I found things as they are."

"He is not dead," said Herbert. " For this I am thankful. Fire a rifle, and bring him back, and the others, too. We can *wait* no longer, but must seek out the cowardly assassins."

Firing a gun from the huts was a pre-arranged signal for all to return with speed, and, David having discharged the weapon, the members of the little band came in with such speed as they could make.

First, John Trevelyn.

Then Sam Gorgon and the boatswain

Then the three seamen, and then—no more.

James Standish did not appear.

In vain they watched for his coming, and listened for his footsteps.   He did not return.

And David Trevelyn knew in his heart that the missing man would never return thither.

"I left him in the house," he said, "and from there they have taken him.   He had no time to get far away, and, having heard the signal, would surely return.   Poor Herbert!"

To look at the youth it would appear that he was not in need of pity.

Standing erect by the door, and leaning on his rifle, he seemed to be quietly awaiting, without any dread or fear, the coming of his father.

But, outwardly composed, he was inwardly suffering a martyrdom, for he felt that his father had been taken from him by the cruel, secret foe, and would never come back to him more.

CHAPTER VII.

THE BURIAL OF CARROLL—A NIGHT OF WATCHING.

WHEN it was quite clear that James Standish had been spirited away alive, or murdered and afterwards removed, his son Herbert asked to be left in peace for awhile, and entering his abode closed the door.   The others were all outside gathered in a group, whispering together about the mystery of the Black Star.

"It's my belief," said Ginger the boatswain, "that the place is harnted.   Maybe old Vanderdecken, the Flying Dutchman, havin' given up a rovin' life at sea, have taken to playing pranks ashore."

"Was there ever such a person as Vanderdecken?" asked David Trevelyn.

"Was—there—iver—such—a pusson—as—Vanderdecken!" repeated Ginger, in a whisper of thrilled astonishment. "Have you ever seen the moon and stars?"

"The moon and the stars can be seen *now*," replied John Trevelyn, taking up the question as if he had introduced it; "but Vanderdecken has never been anything more than the hero of a story."

"A *true* story."

"Well, it may be. I won't dispute it. But I don't think there is anything supernatural about this horrible business."

The three men of the crew appeared to think otherwise.

Spifley looked pityingly at the twin brothers.

"If you young gents had been at sea as long as we have you'd think different. This sperriting away ain't nateral."

"It doesn't seem so," said David; "but for all that I think it will be accounted for by natural means."

"It's somebody with a shop round the corner, and agents in the main thoroughfare," said Sam Gorgon, gloomily. "I've seen something since I took to wandering, but never anything like this."

"I've seen so much," said Ginger, "that nothin' astonishes me. I—"

He stopped short as an expression of the utmost astonishment leaped into his face.

He was standing with his back to the hut, staring between the twin brothers at the wood behind them.

In a few moments all were looking in the same direction, but they could see nothing.

"What was the matter, Mister Ginger?" asked Starbutt.

The boatswain drew a deep breath and passed his hand across his brow.

"I don't know 'zactly what it was," he said; "but summat flashed out of that 'ere bush, turned a whirligig, and vanished."

He pointed to the bush he referred to, and an immediate examination was made of it.

But there was nothing to show that any living man or beast had been near it.

"You must have been mistaken," said John Trevelyn.

"*Me* mistaken—ME!" exclaimed Ginger, as if all creation might go wrong but he would indubitably remain in the right. "Young man, if you'd known me a few years you wouldn't talk in that way."

"Well, what did you see?" asked David.

Ginger was not at all prepared to explain.

"I can't shape it because I didn't make it," he said, adopting a perverse form of logic. "Not knowing what it was I can't be called on for a full explanation; but I SEE it. That's enough for me."

If anybody had been disposed to debate the point with him he would have been debarred doing so.

At that moment the voice of Herbert Standish, quietly asking for the two Trevelyns to come to him, was heard.

They all turned to look at him, and it occurred to one and all that as he stood in the dark doorway he was a very striking figure.

His pose was one of ease.

One hand rested on his hip, the other grasped

the barrel of his rifle, the butt of which stood upon the ground.

On his face was a strange light which did not seem to come from the bright sky above.

It had an awe-inspiring effect upon them all.

" John and David," he said, " will you please come here ?"

The brothers passed through the opening in the *cheveaux de frise,* and the three entered the hut together.

Herbert closed the door.

" I have sent for you," he said, " as I have hope of getting from you in this sore strait the best advice.   First of all, look at this poor fellow who is dead."

Herbert had righted the table, and laid all that remained of poor Carroll upon it.   He had put something under his head for a pillow and composed the limbs.   A perfect calm rested on the face.

" Why, he might be asleep," said David, sympathetically.

" He has not died by ordinary means," returned Herbert ; " for as far as I have been able to discover he has no wounds."

" Is it so ?" exclaimed John.

" It is so," replied Herbert ; " and, what is more, there is a clue to the manner of his death. Do you notice anything peculiar about him ?"

" There is a strange aroma," said David, " and it seems to arise from him generally."

" It is all over him," said Herbert.   " In his hair, upon his clothes and face and hands ; *but it is on nothing else in the place !*"

" Why, this but adds to the mystery," said John ; and David nodded his assent to the proposition.

" The mystery of the disappearance, and this death, must be solved by us," said Herbert.   " We may theorise a little, but we must act promptly.

I have formed some idea of it all, but as yet it is not in shape. Can you suggest anything?"

"Not much," said David. "It seems to me that they have thrown some powerful spirit over him, and that he had died from its effects."

"But if thrown over him some would have been scattered about the floor, and there are no signs of it. I have looked for them everywhere. See how deliberate I have been. You will not, I hope, say that I do not grieve over the loss of my father?"

"Oh! no," exclaimed the brothers together.

"I am not one to waste my breath in words," said Herbert. "Action is the watchword of my race. From this hour I live to rescue my father, if living, and with him, I trust, my ·dear friend, Richard Warden, and if dead, to avenge them. To do one or the other I have need of help. Will you give me yours?"

"With all my heart," said David Trevelyn, as he extended his hand, and John gave his consent by offering his also.

"I will not talk to you of reward," said Herbert, "beyond saying that I hope I shall one day be able to repay you. Now let the rest come in."

David summoned them, and they came filing in quietly, removing their hats as they entered the presence of the dead.

Alive Carroll had not been much of a comrade to them; but in the presence of death the strongest man felt a sensation of weakness and humility.

They stood around the table, and Herbert drew their attention to the fact that no familiar weapon had taken his life; but he insisted that, after all, he had died by natural means.

"He has been drugged," he said, "and died under it; but who administered that drug and how we must find out anon. Here, in the presence of the body of poor Carroll, I ask if you are willing to devote your lives to the discovery of the authors of this crime?"

The answer of all, given in a low, impressive tone, was—

"Yes!"

No question of leadership was mooted.

Herbert took up the position naturally, and as a matter of course, and he was accepted.

Some are born to lead, and they come to the front without any effort of self-assertion.

Rarely, indeed, is the leadership of the natural leader subject to dissent by the majority.

So the little band was formed under Herbert with a clear object, and, in accordance with his disposition, the leader wasted no more time in words.

They buried the gloomy and too prophetic Carroll under a wide-spreading mahogany-tree, and placed a roughly hewn wooden cross to mark his last resting-place.

When that was done they all assembled again to hear what their leader had to give out by the way of orders.

Commands he had none, but he wished to say a few words to them with the object of dispelling all superstitious fears from the hearts of Ginger and the sailors.

David Trevelyn had informed him of the vision the latter had seen a few hours before, and to Ginger he pointedly addressed his few remarks.

"We are not dealing with ghosts or anything supernatural, of that I am assured," he said, "but with some mortal man or body of men, who, for *some powerful reason, object to our presence here.* Now, we must discover who they are and why they object to us.   One thing is certain—that when we *do* know who they are we must fight them, for from this land, as far as I can see, *there is no escape.*

Keep all together to-night," he said ; "and one or more ought to remain on watch.   Decide who it shall be among yourselves ; not until to-morrow will I take full command."

He bade them Good-night, and was turning to his hut, when David Trevelyn asked if he might accompany him.

"No," said Herbert ; "I would be alone to-night as far as man is concerned.   Do not forget I have Nero."

Then he went in and closed the door.

"He doesn't seem to say much about his father," said Ginger, as the men settled round the camp-fire for their evening meal.

"But he thinks all the more," replied Sam Gorgon.   "It isn't always the biggest talkers who feel the keenest."

"You can't tell how much a man feels unless he does talk," said Ginger.

"Well, it's no business of yours, anyway," said Sam Gorgon, shortly.   "Stick to your own line— it's as much as you can attend to."

"Oh ! you think so ?" said Ginger.   "Well, my opinion of you is—   Why, where to goodness is he a-going to ?"

It was John Trevelyn he referred to, who, with his rifle on his shoulder, walked into the wood.

David stood apart from the party round the camp-fire, apparently ignorant of the interest they took in his brother's movements.

He busied himself in examining his rifle, while the rest kept their eyes upon the spot where John had disappeared.

But some minutes elapsed and he did not return.

"Derned if I don't think he's gone a hunting," said Ginger.

"Not he," replied Sam Gorgon.   "Why, it'll be dark in half-an-hour."

"I'll bet he don't come back to-night," said Ginger.

"Done!" said Sam Gorgon; "two plugs of tobacco."

They shook hands upon it, and while they were in the act of sealing their wager, John Trevelyn, came back from the wood exactly at the spot where he had entered.

"Well, I'm blowed if *that* isn't a sell," said Ginger, as he handed out the plug of tobacco. "Seems to me jest as if you'd arranged it atwixt you."

John sauntered up to his brother, and in a quiet way said—

"It is done."

"All round?" asked David.

"Complete—about knee high. No man or beast can intrude this way without leaving signs of their coming behind them."

As it was growing dark the brothers walked up to the camp fire, and after a brief rest and chat with the others the signal was given to all to turn in.

All was soon quiet, and apparently at rest; but though the band might sleep their leader was awake throughout the long night.

Those who exhibit the least grief in public suffer most alone; and with no mortal eye upon him Herbert gave way to his emotion.

First grief assailed him, and it is no shame to his budding manhood that we record the fact of his shedding tears.

Then followed anger, and with clenched hands he marched up and down.

There was no ordinary light in the hut, but from the table on which poor Carroll had briefly lain there was emitted a faint phosphorescent glow, weird and awe-inspiring.

On Nero, the dog, it had the effect of driving him to the far end of the hut, where in a sitting position he stared at it, whining occasionally.

Herbert scarcely glanced at it as he walked to and fro, but occasionally a feeling of fascination drew him towards it.

Once he went up to it, rubbed his fingers in the faint flame, and smelt it.

But the odour apparent on Carroll's clothes was not there.

"It is a mystery," he said—"a mystery; but not for long."

CHAPTER VIII.

THE BROKEN THREADS—A STAR ON HIS BREAST—GOING INTO PERIL.

"Come in !" cried Herbert, as a knock at early dawn came at his door.

David Trevelyn entered.

He looked keenly at Herbert, who sat quietly on one end of the table, carelessly swinging his right leg to and fro.

"You have not slept," he said.

"I sleep when I feel I have need of it," replied Herbert. "Last night all feeling of fatigue was gone. I could not have slept if I had tried. But what brings you so early? The sun is hardly yet risen."

"John and I," replied David, "have been up an hour gathering evidence of night visitors."

"Ah !" exclaimed Herbert, dropping to the ground; "and what have you found ?"

"At least a dozen men came near or into our ground," said John. "Last evening David suggested that I should run a cordon of cotton round the camp, so I took a reel of black from the stores and ran it round the limbs of the trees about knee high. This morning I found it broken in a dozen places from different points. They must have borne down upon us from different directions."

"They did not come here," said Herbert, "for Nero never stirred."

"Well, they have been near us," said Jack, quietly; "and possibly the breaking of the cotton was perceived, and scared them away."

"If I only knew which way to head for," said Herbert, "I should know what to do." He began pacing up and down the room. "But here again we have no guide. If our alarm had come from the north, south, east, or west we could have acted; but it may come from all points. Whoever our foe may be, we have one of great cunning to deal with."

"We must meet cunning with cunning."

"No, John; I'm no hand at that sort of work. I want to know where to find my foe, so as to go out in a manly way and meet him. It galls me—almost maddens me, to think that we must *wait* for him!"

"If they come as wild beasts," said John, "let us treat them as such. Let us watch around, dig pits, and trap, or shoot them."

Herbert did not answer him, but remained a time in deep thought. At last he looked up and said—

"You have not spoken of what you did last night—to the others, I mean?"

"No; they are not yet stirring."

"Well, say nothing, do nothing to disturb them; but at the same time let none stray far away. One thing I am certain of, and that is we must find some good hiding-place for our stores, so that we may desert the camp at a moment's notice. Can I leave this to you?"

"I will gladly undertake it," was the reply.

David was outside kicking together the stray wood so as to start the morning fire.   That done he roused the rest, and in a little while they came out to perform their ablutions near the spring.

"Nothing come nigh us last night," said Ginger, as he rubbed some soap round his neck.   "I kep' awake for hours on the lookout."

"You mean you kept us awake with your snoring," replied Sam Gorgon.

"What, ME !—*snoring !*" exclaimed Ginger.

"It was the most awful row I ever heard in my life," said Sam.

"Did any of you ever hear me snore ?" asked Ginger, appealing to the three seamen.

"Well, you don't exzactly snore," replied Tomlinson, with a sly wink at the other two, "but now and then you makes *a kind o' nosey sound.* 'Taint unpleasant—when you are used to it."

"You hear that ?" said Ginger to Sam Gorgon.

"Oh ! yes ; I hear," returned Sam.   "All I can say is that if snores were a marketable article I'd like to work the old country with a few of yours for samples.   I'll bet I'd do a roaring trade."

"Oh ! blow your trade," said Ginger, gruffly ; and then Starbutt, Tomlinson, and Spifley went to work washing their heads and spluttering just as if they wished to ward off a fit of laughter.

Tomlinson was a tall, powerfully-built fellow of middle life, with a somewhat wild expression when excited.

As a rule he was an easy-going fellow, but his comrades said that when roused he was a dangerous man to deal with.

We have entered into this description of the man because he was that day the hero, or victim, of a very startling adventure.

After breakfast John Trevelyn started out to find some place wherein to hide a portion or the whole of their stores.

It was suggested by his young leader that he should go towards the sea as the most unlikely direction for a foe to be met with.

The hand that painted the Black Star upon the door of one hut and floor of another would assuredly not be found seaward.

Herbert remained behind, and having given directions to the men remaining about packing certain things, sat down upon the stump of a tree to think out some feasible plan of action.

Nero reclined at his feet, and Sam Gorgon went to and fro bearing messages to the men.

Sam was not exactly in a happy frame of mind. He was sure there was something in the air which might demand very prompt and aggressive action from him.

With a view to being "on the spot ready for a bit of business," as he termed it, he carried his rifle with him wherever he went.

As a shot he was not quite a prize marksman, but he was sure that if the foe, whoever that foe might be, would only show up in sufficient numbers, and keep sufficiently close together to give a novice a chance, that he would hit some of them.

He had been to and fro for an hour and a half or thereabouts, and was standing behind Herbert, when a wild-eyed man suddenly burst from the wood.

It was Tomlinson, the seaman, looking for all the world as if suddenly bereft of his senses.

"Oh ! captain," he cried.   "Save me !"

He stood erect, with his hands clasped before him, with such a terror upon him as Herbert had never seen or known before.

Tomlinson was not by any means a coward.

His record as a seaman was a good one, and stories to his credit had been told of his bearing during the wreck.

To his coolness, it was said, Ginger, the boatswain, owed his life, for when that worthy lost his head it was Tomlinson who stood on the deck of the shivering vessel beside him, and bound him to a hencoop, which was eventually the means of carrying him ashore.

But now the man seemed to be bereft of his senses.

"Come, come," said Herbert, in his calm way. "Don't go on so.   What are you afraid of?"

"This!" shrieked Tomlinson, as he tore open the front of his shirt and exhibited the ominous Black Star.

There it was, painted in the same crude fashion and of the same material, and the sight of the star was a bit of a shock to Herbert.

"How came it there?" he asked.

"I don't know," hoarsely replied Tomlinson, as he glanced hurriedly about him, as if fearing to see some dreaded foe.

"That is idle talk, Tomlinson."

"No, captain, it ain t.   I'll tell you how it was, as far as I can.   I left with Mr. Trevelyn, as you know, and we went on through the wood together until we came in sight of the sea.   Then I stopped to pick up something I saw on the ground, and Mr. Trevelyn went on."

"Well, what did you see?"

"I don't know, for I never picked it up.   It glittered, and I stooped to touch it.   Something came over me like—like an extinguisher."

"And then?"

"I knowed no more until I woke up, not *far from here*, and found myself lying with my shirt front open with this 'ere thing on my breast."

"Tomlinson, if you are playing some trick—"

"Captain, do I look like a man up to anything of the sort? No! The devils have put their mark on me, and I'm a doomed man."

His eyes fairly bulged out of his head, so alarmed was the man. Herbert took him by the arm and bade him compose himself.

"I can fight and die like a man," he said, "but I can't put up with what ain't nateral. It's a haunted land—full o' such fiends who spirit away poor chaps to keep 'em in everlasting torment."

"Tomlinson," said our hero, sternly, "have done with such rubbish. Where is Mr. Trevelyn?"

"I ain't seen him."

"But surely he missed you, and would turn back to see what had become of you?"

"What 'd be the good o' that—when the spirits can make themselves invisible, and if—"

Herbert checked him with an impatient movement.

"I tell you, man," he said, "that there are neither fiends, nor witches, nor hobgoblins in the matter, but men who have some object in scaring and driving us away from here. Pluck up a heart. Where is your rifle?"

"I dropped it, I suppose," replied Tomlinson, feebly.

"Get another," said Herbert, "and come with me. I will show to you how little there is to fear."

"You put a heart in me," said Tomlinson, with a sigh, "but it's mighty skeering. I don't see how it is done."

"Nor could you see how a conjuring trick is performed," said Herbert. "Cover up your breast. Gorgon, say nothing about this for the present."

"Very well, sir," answered Sam Gorgon,

The sight of the star on Tomlinson's breast was a bit of a shock to Herbert

faintly; "but I agree with Tomlinson that it's a bit of a lifter."

"Find Mr. David Trevelyn, and send him to me," said Herbert.

David was not far away, and soon obeyed the summons. Herbert drew him aside and told him what had happened.

"I am going to see that your brother is not in trouble," he added.

"He is not in trouble," replied David, quietly.

"How do you know that?"

"Because I should be in trouble, too. Minor sensations we have not in common, but any great pain felt by one is known to the other."

"I have heard of such things," said Herbert, "and could not believe them."

"You can believe it now," said David, "for it is true with us whatever it may have been with others."

"But if I do not go to him he may get into trouble," urged Herbert. "I leave you in charge here. We shall speedily return."

"As you wish. It is kind—noble—of you to do so much."

"Tomlinson, are you ready?"

"Ay! captain."

The man had now got over his terror, and was braced up for a struggle with any ordinary foe.

He had found another rifle which he was engaged in loading.

"Let us hasten," said Herbert.

He strode away, followed by Tomlinson. Nero would have gone too, but his master commanded him to return.

With a wistful look and a whine he obeyed.

David Trevelyn returned to his interrupted labours and Sam Gorgon was left alone.

"H'm!" he muttered. "I am not invited to

go. The captain doesn't believe in me. Well, I'm not so plucky as some, but I can show fight at a pinch. Am I afraid of the Black Star party? I don't know. Am I afraid of losing my life in a good cause? I don't think so. Anyway, here goes to follow the captain, and maybe I'll get a chance of rushing into the rescue. Fancy! Sam G., agent for anything that anyone will entrust him with to sell, and I used to think travelling hard lines, but I'd like to be on the old home roads again. Heigho!"

He paused a moment, thinking deeply, and then with a sudden resolute movement he looked up.

"Captain," he said, half-aloud, "you're bound to get into trouble I know it, I feel it, and Sam Gorgon is on his way to save you."

With a flourish of his arm he announced his resolution to the men around, but nobody was looking at him, and unheeded he plunged into the wood.

Sam Gorgon half repented of his daring as soon as he got well within the shadow of the wood; he wholly repented of it when he had traversed a hundred yards.

But he did not go back.

"What you've got to do, Sam," he said, softly, "is to fight against that coward heart of your'n. You can't help being born with it; but, like all things, it can be improved upon. Hark! what's that?"

He stopped short and listened.

The sound which fell upon his ears was like the fluttering of many wings, interspersed with a soft, tingling sound.

As far as he could judge it came from afar off.

"Now, I wonder," said Sam, as he felt a kind of trickling sensation down his back (it was his courage going down into his boots)—" I wonder if this is an enchanted land ?   Whew ! it's coming."

The tinkling and the fluttering sounds increased, and Sam, with a sudden resolve to save his life, if possible, looked about him for a hiding-place."

The trunk of one huge mahogany tree near him was hollow, and close to the ground there was a hole just about big enough for a man to creep into.

Sam thrust his gun in and followed with all speed.

The interior was a foot thick with pungent dust, almost as bad as snuff to the eyes and nostrils.

The small cloud he raised set Sam sneezing, and the row he made—much against his will—was sufficient to be heard a quarter of a mile off.

Oh ! how he confounded it ; but, like many other ills of life, he had to keep quiet under its influence or suffer all the more.

At last there was not a sneeze left in him, and sitting as still as a mouse he listened intently for the fluttering and tinkling sounds.

Both had ceased.

The wood was, for a brief space of time, absolutely still.

He was beginning to think that he might emerge again when a rustling among the undergrowth outside fell upon his attentive ears.

It was away to the left, and without putting his head out he could not see what it was.   This put him on tenter-hooks.

" Somebody prowling around and looking for ME," he thought.

Whoever it was had come close to the tree, and had either sat down or was standing still.

Sam judged by the silence that he, she, or they were listening.

" The next they will do," he thought, " will be

to LOOK. Hang it! why did I ever get into this hole?"

His rifle was standing barrel up, and the hollow was not wide enough to enable him to reverse it, so as to bring the muzzle to bear upon his foe.

Sam felt quite at his mercy.

"I've messed the whole business," he thought; "but when a man takes to travelling out of his line he's bound to do something wrong. England— home of my birth—farewell! Here they come! All I can do is to give the first one a prod with the butt of my gun, and then it will be all over with me."

He nervously grasped his rifle, intending to lower it so that he might give the enemy some sort of blow with the butt of it.

CHAPTER IX.

SAM GORGON FINDS THINGS NOT SO BAD AS HE FEARED—A NEW STOREHOUSE.

SAM unhappily laid hold of the trigger and gave it a pull.

Down it went, and—

Bang!

Well, it was not so much of a bang as a thunderous roar, and, to Sam's imagination, a kind of upheaval of nature all-round.

The cloud of dust from the rotting tree that came down upon him was fearful, and in addition he dislodged a nest of wasps or bees or some sort of stinging insects, which fell upon him and at once entered upon the work of vengeance.

The way they stung him about the head and ears drove all thoughts of other perils out of his head.

Regardless of anything and everything but the necessity of immediately getting out of his present difficulty at any cost, he dashed head first out of the hold, and the moment he was half outside an iron hand pinned him by the nape of the neck and held him fast.

Sam Gorgon felt himself dragged along in the most unceremonious manner, while somebody in good solid English confounded him for a fool.

In his confused state of mind and agony, arising from the stings he received from the dislodged insects, he did not recognise the voice. Great was his astonishment then when he was suddenly turned over on his back, and saw John Trevelyn standing over him.

"What were you doing inside that tree?" demanded John. "It's a wonder I didn't put a bullet through you."

"Oh! it's you, is it?" said Sam, dismally. "Get away, will you!"

The latter words were addressed to a waspish-looking insect that made an effort to settle on Sam's nose.

It was one of the avenging host from which John Trevelyn had dragged him away.

"Yes, it's me. I was coming back to camp," was the reply. "I want to know why Tomlinson skulked back again."

"I've got a staggerer for you," said Sam.

And then he told John the story of Tomlinson's adventure.

With a very grave face the young fellow listened to him without interrupting with a single word. When Sam had finished he simply said—

"We had better go and find the captain. He may get into trouble looking for me."

"I'll get my gun first, if you don't mind," said Sam. "I left it inside that tree. I wonder if there are any of these beastly stingers about?"

"They went sailing aloft in a little cloud,"

replied John, laughing.   " But be sharp.   If they should drop upon you there are sufficient to sting you to death."

Sam had a good look around, and then with extreme caution walked on tip-toe to the hollow of the tree.

The butt of his gun was sticking out, and grasping it, he gave the weapon a jerk that brought it down with a run, followed by a liberal allowance of dust.

Sam thought another supply of his stinging enemies had come forth, and the way he ran was a sight indeed.

" Stop—stop !" cried John, as he darted by. " It's only dust this time."

" I'm thankful for that," replied Sam, pulling up ; " but one dose of stinging is enough.   What is my face like ?"

" A very ripe, prickly, enormous gooseberry," replied John.

" It seems to be swelling," said Sam, dolorously. " Hang the little pests !"

John led the way, retracing his steps to the sea, where he found Herbert and Tomlinson looking anxiously for him.

" I was afraid something had happened to you," said Herbert, " especially after this affair of Tomlinson's.   Of course Gorgon has told you about it ?"

" He has," replied John Trevelyn.   " It's an odd affair, but I do not think we may be alarmed about it."

" I am not alarmed," said Herbert, quietly.

" I didn't exactly mean that," said John.   " Now I'm inclined to think that a form of practical joking is going on."

" Rather serious joking for me," said Tomlinson.   " Have you seen such paint as this in your life? I can feel it eating into me. I've got a mark on me which I'll have to carry through life."

He opened his breast and exhibited the star again.

Truly it had the appearance of being branded into his flesh.

"Does it pain you?" asked Sam.

"No," replied Tomlinson; "but for all that I can feel the star *settling down into my skin!* It will hold to me like good tattooing."

"Whoever puts the mark on," said Herbert, "seems to know how to make it indelible. On the floor at home it sticks as if no human power could remove it."

"Indelible and indestructible paint," murmured Sam Gorgon. "What a trade I could do in it at home! What a rush there would be on it!"

"You seem to have a good eye to business," remarked John Trevelyn.

"It's the only thing my eye is good for," sighed Sam.

Now that they were together Herbert suggested that the original object—looking for a good hiding-place for their stores—should be carried out.

"But whether we can hide anything from our invisible foe is an open question," said John.

"We can try," said Herbert.

On Tomlinson, the seaman, was a strange calm.

He spoke and looked as if he was a doomed man and was now fully resigned to his fate.

This was not to be wondered at under the circumstances, for no man likes dealing with an invisible and incomprehensible foe.

They wandered on for about two miles, and then they came to the mouth of a river which was very narrow near the sea.

On either side of it were high rocks for half-a-mile inland. Beyond that distance the stream was wider, and as the water flowed swiftly the rush through the gorge formed by the precipitous cliffs was tremendous.

"With the tide running out," said John Trevelyn, "no boat would ever get in."

"I doubt if there is any backward flow here," replied Herbert, "for there seems to me to be a tremendously swift rush of water from the mountains."

"And it is the dry season now evidently. What will it be like when the rain falls?"

They followed the upward course of the river until they came to a broken part of the bank, and then they found what promised to be a secure hiding-place for their stores.

It was a sloping shaft going into the ground at an angle of about forty-five degrees, and at first appeared to be of considerable depth.

Herbert boldly entered it to explore, and the others followed with a feeling that they were going to throw themselves into the arms of an enemy.

But when their eyes got used to the gloom they saw that the shaft abruptly terminated about thirty yards from its entrance, and what was very strange was the fact that it widened out internally so as to be funnel-shaped.

"The very place," said Herbert. "We could stow here ten times the amount of things we have, and the mouth being narrow we can easily block it with stones. A little earth and a few wild flowers planted will give it a natural appearance."

"But we must disturb them to get what we want," suggested Sam Gorgon.

"I propose to keep out a fortnight's ammunition and rations of biscuit," said Herbert. "For the rest we must rely upon our guns."

"And how will you spend that fortnight?" asked John Trevelyn.

"Moving here and there, but not going far away—camping in different places, and watching and waiting for this sneaking foe, who comes and goes like an evil shadow. Let the work of removal begin at once ; I will remain here."

"Alone ?"

"Yes. Why not ? It is broad daylight, and I can see all around me. Have no fear for me, as I have none for myself."

But alone they would not leave him, and Tomlinson remained behind to keep him company, while Sam Gorgon and John Trevelyn returned to the camp.

CHAPTER X.

THE STRANGE FOOTSTEPS—STORING IN THE SHAFT—VANISHED.

HERBERT and Tomlinson sat down by the mouth of the sloping shaft, which was one of the most elevated parts of the high ground.

From this place they could command a view of a considerable stretch of sea, beach, wood, and the varied landscape inland.

No mortal foe could approach unseen.

Herbert was in no talking mood, and Tomlinson had been reduced to a state of unusual quietude by his adventure, so that both were silent for some time.

Herbert fell into a train of thought that led him from surrounding things.

From this he was aroused by a hand being laid upon his arm.

Looking up he saw that Tomlinson was bending over to him, and as a signal to be silent had a finger on his nether lip.

With the slightest possible motion of his head,

Tomlinson indicated that he wished to draw the attention of his leader to the interior of the shaft.

Without moving his head Herbert directed his hearing to that place, and to his utter amazement heard a sound that was like the pattering of naked feet upon a stone floor.

He cast a quick glance at his rifle, and, seeing that it was cocked and ready for use, he seized it and sprang to his feet.

"Don't go in, for Heaven's sake ! sir," implored Tomlinson.

"You stand here," replied Herbert, "and shoot anybody strange who attempts to fly out. I have had enough of this fooling. No really brave or powerful foe will descend to these tricks."

With a resolute look upon his face he strode into the shaft, and, with his rifle ready for use, half-walked, half-slid down to the very end.

He encountered—nobody !

Placing his back against the wall of stone, he stared up the funnel.

Certainly no living thing save himself was within it.

Despite his natural courage he felt a bit creepy. It was certainly an addition to the other mysteries of his life in this strange land.

Might it not be possible that he had to deal with the supernatural ?

His education and training made him averse to the thought ; but he could not quite ignore it.

"I will swear I heard footsteps here, within this cave," he muttered.

Slowly retracing his steps he searched right and left to find some clue to the mystery, but there was none.

Outside he found Tomlinson anxiously awaiting his return.

"You've found nothing, sir ?"

"No."

"I didn't think you would. I tell you, sir, we've got to a harnted land. Mr. Ginger, and Starbutt, and Spifley, and me have made up our minds to *that*, whatever you may think of it."

"It may be so," said Herbert; "but I must have some stronger evidence ere I believe it."

"Who—o—o—o—o !"

It was a faint cry that fell upon their startled ears; but the direction from whence it came was unmistakable.

It was from the shaft.

They both drew aside, and Tomlinson's head sank upon his breast.

Clasping his hands, he shivered from crown to heel.

"We are all doomed men," he muttered.

Raising his head he looked piteously at Herbert.

"Couldn't we knock up some sort of boat and get away from here?" he asked.

"You may all go if you like," replied Herbert, "and I will not blame you; but here *I* remain to learn the mystery of my father's fate."

"It's very 'fine to talk," groaned Tomlinson; "but you've got to do it."

He sat down upon the ground, and resting his elbows upon his knees, clasped his head with his hands.

The poor fellow was the very image of despair.

Herbert did not reproach him, for he knew that many would have yielded to the same emotion under the circumstances.

Presently Ginger and Starbutt appeared, each with a big bundle of stores strapped to his broad shoulders.

By their faces Herbert could see that they had heard about Tomlinson.

"It seems to me a waste o' time to shift these

things, sir," said Ginger, "for fly where you may you can't get clear of speerits."

"Place your packages here," said Herbert, quietly. "I will store them in the shaft."

"It's a good thing as you can take things so cool, sir," replied Ginger, "for I've heard say as a speerit won't tackle a man as ain't afeard of it. When my father seed Maria Barber's ghost on Clapham Common he stood up to it and hit out like a man; but it didn't happen to be Maria's ghost that time, although it had been seen every night for a month afore."

"And what was it, Mister Ginger?" asked Tomlinson.

"It was a neighbour as was going home from he market," replied Ginger; "and what with the row she made, and the policeman coming and locking father up, and his being fined two pounds and called a fool by the magistrates in the morning, my poor old father had a bad time of it."

"Then it wasn't a ghost," said Starbutt, "and it's no credit to him for standing up against it."

"But he *thought* it was," said Ginger, "and the feeling is just the same."

Up to sunset the work of removing stores went on, and by that time the greater portion had been transferred to the shaft.

All that day Herbert kept watch for the signs of a spying foe and saw none.

In addition to his eyes, in the afternoon he used the powerful ship's glass which had been saved from the wreck.

With it he swept both land and sea, and never once made out anything in the form of a man.

Away on the plain he saw two or three herds of deer pass by, and once he saw some black dots moving on one of the distant hills.

What these latter were he did not make out, for

as he was focussing his glass for the distance **they** disappeared.

They closed up the mouth of the shaft, and, leaving it for the night, returned to their old camp to sleep.

All through the night Nero was very restless, and was constantly sniffing at the door ; but when Herbert arose and opened it he refused to go out.

Herbert went forth two or three times with his rifle at the ready and took a quiet look around.

But he saw nothing save a few faint, flickering lights dancing in the wood, which he judged were fire-flies, of which there were many visible every night.

He was glad when the dawn came.

First they all had a morning meal of biscuit and meat, then rations of biscuit for a fortn'ght were served out to each man.

Last of all they were given fifty rounds of ammunition apiece.

The rest was packed up so as to be secure from damp, and this and the rest of the goods when equally divided made a moderate burden for each man.

They all knew of Herbert's intention to keep shifting here and there, and even that form of action was pleasing to them.

Nothing is more wearying and depressing in war than *waiting* for a foe.

And our friends were practically at war with that most dreaded of enemies—the unseen.

There was the element of relief in any form of action, and the spirits of all sensibly rose as they set out in a body for the shaft by the river.

Even Tomlinson, burdened with the fatal brand, lost some of his gloom, and talked a little with real or assumed cheerfulness.

As for Nero, he bounded on before, barking joyously as he had not done for many days.

The high land was reached, and they stood around the mouth of the shaft.

Before touching it Herbert examined the big stones which had been used to block the entrance.

He had carefully noted them the night before, and he was sure they had not been touched.

Ginger and the seamen rolled them away, and Herbert entered the shaft.

With a steady step he descended and reached the bottom to find—nothing !

All the things stored away on the previous day had disappeared.

CHAPTER XI.

MYSTERY ON MYSTERY—WHERE IS THE SAVAGE ?—A RISKY DESCENT.

A FEELING of sickness came over Herbert. The whole thing was so mysterious and so terribly serious.

Fully five-sixths of his useful stores had been stolen.

With a palpable foe to meet he would have cared little, but with this silent, crafty, and strange enemy, what was he to do?

How would those outside bear the dire intelligence?

He could see them moving to and fro, talking together, and at the mouth of the shaft lay Nero, who had declined to follow his master into its gloom.

"I'll not believe that anything more than man is doing these things," said Herbert, "and they must be brought to think so too."

Bracing himself up to tell them the direful news,

he went, and in a few calm words enlightened them about their new misfortune.

They heard him in silence, but the effect of it was but too apparent in the minds of all.

To get away from the unhallowed spot.

"It is useless to disguise from you," said Herbert, "that I am completely at sea as to the nature of the enemy we are dealing with. Choose your own answer now. It has been suggested to me that a boat should be made, and be taken to the sea. What say you?"

"Can we do any good by remaining here?" asked David Trevelyn.

"No," said the others.

"You have your axes and the materials to make a boat," said Herbert; "but I cannot help you, as I do not understand such labour. Who among you will undertake to superintend it?"

Ginger said he had worked in a ship-yard before he went to sea, and knew how to put a boat "on the stocks," and he was elected as foreman.

Sam Gorgon also declared his inability to do anything, so he and Herbert elected to provide meat for the community.

At once the work was entered upon, and Ginger, having selected a few useful half-grown trees, the others went to work, cutting them down.

"Come, Sam," said Herbert, "we must find some distraction for our minds. We will go hunting."

Taking Nero with them they started along the river's course, where they hoped to find tracks of animals who came down at night to drink.

The banks were very rugged, and they proceeded very slowly. While still within sight of the gorge another of the strange series of adventures befell them.

On a floating log stood the statue-like form of a magnificent savage.

They were standing on a jutting rock by the river, it was at the bend, when Nero uttered a short, sharp bark, and then took up a pointer-like attitude, staring up the stream.

They followed his fixed gaze for a few moments and saw nothing.

Then round the bend came a strange apparition. On a floating log stood, with statue-like ease, the form of a magnificent savage.

In his left hand he held a bow, on his back was a quiver, and in his right hand was a banner of woven grass.

On the latter was the ominous sign of the Black Star.

The rapid stream brought the log swiftly down.

The savage never stirred.

Even his eyes were fixed, and he went by like a thing without life, staring at them as he floated past, and yet without apparently seeing them.

So strange a spectacle had a very awe-inspiring effect upon the two spectators.

They stood as still as the savage, and he had come and gone ere Herbert thought of the rifle he carried in his hand.

When it flashed upon him that he had the means of bringing this stranger down, the log had disappeared within the gorge.

"Up to the top of the cliff!" shouted Herbert, bravely.

He was as nimble as a first-class athlete, and soon outstripped Sam Gorgon in the race for the summit, from whence a view of the water in the gorge to the sea could be obtained.

But when Herbert reached the top, neither log nor savage were in sight.

Our hero ran to a point where he could see the whole mouth of the river and the sea to the right and left.

But nothing out of the ordinary way met his view.

The statuesque savage on his rugged raft had vanished as if he had been but a dream.

It is not easy to describe the emotion which Herbert felt in making this discovery.

The daring savage might have fallen off and been drowned, but where was the log?

That at least would float, and ought to have been visible in the rushing river or in the placid sea.

He threw himself down, and hung over the rocks until he was in danger of falling over.

Sam Gorgon, almost out of breath, came running up and begged of him not to run so terrible a risk, for few men could have fallen into the stream below and successfully battled with its turbid waters.

" I want to find out what has become of him," said Herbert, hotly. " This jugglery—for I sure it is nothing more—maddens me."

" What did *you* see?" asked Sam.

" A savage on a log, with a bow and banner of woven grass."

" Just what I saw; but it didn't seem real to me."

Sam's face was as white as a sheet, and even Nero with his tail well between his legs came crawling up as if he too were thoroughly nonplussed and beaten.

The faces of the steep banks were not entirely smooth.

Here and there they were broken up, and in two or three places huge rocks hung over the stream.

It was possible that the savage and his crude raft might be under one of these.

But how did he manage to remain there?

What man, single-handed, could hold a thing fast against that mighty rush of water ?

The noise it made was like that of an engine letting off steam.

It eddied and swirled and foamed.   The pace of it was tremendous.

"Sam," said Herbert, "I am going to try to get down this rock. There is some sort of foothold, and I am an old hand at cliff climbing."

"For mercy's sake, don't attempt it !" cried Sam, "there isn't foothold enough for a cat."

"Foothold or not," said Herbert between his teeth, "I'm going to attempt it."

He tossed off his hat and began kicking off his boots as he spoke.   Sam wrung his hands in an agony of fear.

"We shall lose you," he said, "and then we might just as well all jump into this river and put an end to the whole business."

Herbert did not heed him.

Having divested himself of his vest and laid aside his shot-belt and other things that might impede his downward descent, he took another steady look at the stone wall below him and then slowly lowered himself half-way until he found his feet resting on a small piece of protruding rock.

"Now keep quiet, Gorgon," he said, "and don't make any fuss.   The less noise there is the better I shall get on."

Nero at this moment came whining up to his master, as if he, too, expostulated against his risking his life.

Herbert gently patted the noble brute upon the head.

"Good-bye, old fellow—for the present," he said.

Sam Gorgon expostulated no more.

Quietly he put Herbert's things together and sat down beside them.

"If you will go, you must," he said; "but I think it possible to be born with too much courage."

Herbert held out his hand.

"If anything happens to me, Gorgon," he said, "you will go back to the fellows and tell them that my last hope was that they might get out of this accursed country—safe back to their homes and friends."

Sam Gorgon shook his head and turned his face away.

"They will lose all heart without you!" he said.

"Not with the two Trevelyns," he said; "they have their heads screwed on the right way. You know the old adage: 'Two heads are better than one.'"

He spoke in a light, jesting tone, but Sam was not comforted.

"There are not two heads like yours!" he said.

"Well, shake hands," said Herbert, "just as a matter of form."

Sam grasped his hand, and Herbert felt a drop of water fall upon it. His simple companion was affected to tears.

Herbert made no comment upon it, but he, too, was deeply moved.

Knowing he had need of all his nerve he began his descent.

As Sam Gorgon had said, there was barely toot-hold for a cat; but Herbert had muscles of steel, and as a cliff-climber had made his mark in his boyhood.

It used to be said of him that the greatest joy of his life was to risk being dashed to pieces, and his happiness would never be complete until he had succeeded in doing it.

Holding on with a wonderful tenacity he descended, feeling his way step by step, his whole form glued to the rock, and his hands and feet shifting with caution slowly.

The upper part of his journey was the most dangerous.

Half-way down there was a rock about the size of one of the old-fashioned round dining-tables.

If he reached that he would be able to rest himself and be comparatively safe.

He could not see it as he descended, because he could not turn his head to look downwards ; but he judged the distance as well as he could, and drew a deep breath of relief as each step brought him nearer to it.

But he was so long reaching it that it seemed to him that it glided down as he descended.

This, of course, was only an effect upon an overstrained mind.

The rock remained firm in its place.

But man's endurance, though great, has a limit, and Herbert soon began to find that his strength was yielding to the strain.

" I can't hold on much longer," he thought ; " how far is it ?"

He felt his whole strength going.

A feeling of his muscles being fairly torn out of their fleshy beds came upon him. The agony he felt was unendurable.

The impulse to turn his head and look down was irresistible.

He had only bent it half way over his right shoulder when the stone wall slipped from his grasp, his whole figure bent backward, and with a smothered groan upon his lips he fell.

Sam Gorgon did not attempt to watch his leader during his descent.

To the simple business man it was an appalling,

impossible feat to carry out, and the destruction of his leader was in his opinion certain.

Hence the stillness that came over him.

It was the quietude of despair.

Seated on the ground, with the subdued Nero by his side, he listened to the slow scrape—scrape which marked his leader's descent, like one who is awaiting the signal of death of a dear friend.

"He can't get down—he will be dashed to pieces."

CHAPTER XII.

HERBERT FINDS A DOUBLE CAVE—THE APPARITION—MEN OR FIENDS?

HERBERT, when he lost his hold of the cliff-side, fell with considerable force on the projecting rock below, and for awhile lay half-stunned but not imperfectly conscious of what had happened.

When he recovered sufficiently to realise his position Sam Gorgon was well on his way to the spot where the boat building was going on, and Nero had followed him.

Herbert's first thought was to examine himself to see if any bones were broken, and was considerably relieved to find that, as far as his limbs were concerned, he had received no material injury.

A bruise or two hardly counted with him, but in a general way he felt the shock he had received.

He was, in short, a bit upset, and had lost half his usual nerve.

But enough of his original pluck remained to urge him on to the completion of his task, which was to get down and see what was under that overshadowing rock.

That could not be done at the head of it; but at the side, where it was connected with the cliff, he found sufficient foot and hand-hold to enable him to resume his way.

Before starting he called to Sam Gorgon by name, and found a further element of disturbance in not getting an answer.

"I suppose he has run away," he thought. "Well, alone I will go through with it all!"

The descent was now easier than heretofore, and the daring young adventurer was soon in a position to see under the rock.

He expected to find the savage with his crude raft there, but neither was in sight.

But there was something to account for their disappearance.

Side by side were the entrances to two small caves, both so dark that their penetration into the earth to a considerable distance was a certainty.

By the mouth of one there was a broad ledge of stone—a natural landing-stage, but into the other the water poured with comparative silence but tremendous velocity.

Down the latter the savage on his log might have disappeared.

But whither had he gone?

To what secret cavern of the earth had the rushing water borne him?

That it found a free passage beyond the mouth of this cave was certain, for the rapid river divided itself there, and poured fully a third of its swiftly-rushing water into that dark orifice.

"Well, if you went *that* way, my friend," said Herbert, "I can't follow you; but I can see what is inside the other place."

He got upon the landing-stage, as we may call it, without any great difficulty, and for a few moments stood facing the dark mouth of the cave, endeavouring to pierce its gloom with his eyes.

But the interior was as black as the entrance to

Hades; and if Herbert hesitated for a brief space of time before attempting to enter there was nothing strange in it.

Who in his place would not have done the same?

He was not unarmed, for he had a revolver in his pocket, and it occurred to him that he had better examine it before venturing into the cave.

Ere he could do so a startling phenomenon presented itself at the mouth of the cave.

Out of the dense darkness emerged a robed figure, or skeleton rather, for there was the grinning skull, and a bony hand was extended towards him in a warning way.

Herbert staggered back a pace, and narrowly escaped falling into the swift, flowing river.

The whole thing was so startling and so sudden, and just then he was, as we know, minus some of his accustomed nerve.

But he shook off the momentary terror, and thrust his hand into his pocket.

Skeleton or not, he meant to test its nature with a bullet, but in an instant it was gone.

Swiftly and silently as it came it disappeared.

"I am not to be terrified by your jugglery, whoever you are," cried Herbert. "Come out and show yourself."

No answer was vouchsafed him. With a stern, immovable face, he waited for any additional appearance, but none arrived.

All was still, save the restless river, which rushed and eddied and swirled here and there with many varieties of sound, all, however, in the minor key—soft and subdued.

Herbert was resolved not to be daunted by the startling figure he had seen.

If of this earth, why should he fear it? If of the other, he did not dread its power.

",The devil may play pranks," he muttered, " but he cannot keep a hold on me for ever."

So saying, he drew his revolver, and boldly entered the cave.

By the direction it took he saw at once that it diverged at a considerable angle from the cavern into which the water ran, and they were therefore, so far as the entrance went, distinct underground passages.

Pausing for a few seconds to get his eyes accustomed to the gloom, Herbert kept his ears upon the stretch to catch the slightest sound ahead.

But no vault beneath a church, or the tomb of kings, was more still than that cave.

" How far does it go ?" muttered Herbert, as he cautiously renewed his forward movement.

It bore away to the left for a few yards, then round to the right, and there the darkness was so terrible that it stood up like a wall of black marble before him.

" Shall I go on ?" was his natural thought ; "and if I do what good purpose can I serve ?   Is it here where I shall find a solution of the mystery of the Black Star ?"

He did not like the idea of going back, but he felt that it would be rash to go on alone, and yet, why not?

" Only a little further," he said, softly, " and then if there is nothing but this blackness I will return."

Two steps forward he took and stopped, for out of the gloom came a series of discordant sounds as if a thousand fiends had been let loose upon him.

Such cries, groans, yells, and moans he had never heard nor conceived.

Then suddenly there was a flash of light, brief as the glare of the electric fluid. It revealed to him a score of gibbering faces close upon him ; one, indeed, was within a few inches of him.

After the flash the darkness was as deep as before, and the cries of the occupants of the cave, whoever they might be, ceased.

Herbert stood his ground.

" Men or devils !" he cried, " I do not fear you. Do your worst !"

" Away !" shrieked a score of voices.

" Ha ! my own tongue," said Herbert, with a laugh. " That tells me you are no savage people. Have done with your antics and let me know who you are.

There was no answer ; again silence, deep and impressive, reigned within the cave.

" I must know what it all means," thought Herbert. " I will go on."

Stepping lightly, he advanced half-a-dozen paces, and then from the darkness above something fell upon him like a net and enveloped him in its folds.

It was of some horrible clinging material, like a huge cobweb, and the touch of it upon his face and hands sent a thrill of horror through him.

But it was stronger than a thousand cobwebs, and held him close in its uncanny embrace.

He struggled to release himself, and ound that it had him secure in its clasp.

Then he was drawn over and rolled upon the ground by some invisible power.

Had he been conscious of the touch of a human hand he would have borne it courageously enough, but to be held within such a horrible net and twisted and turned about by an unseen and unrecognisable hand was too much for him.

One loud shout for help burst from his lips, and he was answered by a roar of derision.

Then he was hurried on—through the air, as it

seemed to him—on and on for a good hundred yards or more.

A sudden halt was made, and he was dropped unceremoniously to the ground.

" Lie there and perish," shrieked a harsh voice, followed by a sound like the flapping of huge bat-like wings.

After that—silence.

CHAPTER XIII.

THE ALARM AT THE CAMP—UNAVAILING SEARCH FOR HERBERT—THE BRAND AGAIN—STRANGE CONDUCT OF THE DOG NERO.

" I THINK," said Ginger, " that the lines o' this ere boat want to be on the good old principle—not too great a depth o' keel, but broad on the beam."

" That, of course, is for you to decide," replied John Trevelyn, " for you are boss of the ship-yard."

" And a better boss couldn't be found," said Tomlinson; " he is a man, is Mister Ginger, as ought to ha' been Admiral o' the Fleet or Prime-heir o' England, and he'd ha' done his duty well."

" Do you think you could build this 'ere boat better than me?" asked Ginger, with strained politeness.

" No, I don't," replied Tomlinson.

" Then don't you give me none o' your chaff and cheek," said Ginger, " for I knows the worth of it."

" No offence, Mister Ginger, I hopes."

" Not yet, but just you and them two lazy pals o' yours go to work with the saw and cut off the supuffluous branches from that 'ere tree."

He pointed to a trunk which they had recently

felled, and the men, muttering compliments or something in that way on Ginger and his "airs," set to work.

The brothers Trevelyn assisted Ginger in putting together two rugged trestles, which were to be part of a bench to work upon.

They were debating with Ginger about the height thereof, when Sam Gorgon's voice was heard in the distance.

Looking up, they saw him advancing as if he had acquired possession of the seven-leagued boots of ancient fable, and by his side Nero was running in a half-hearted, dejected style.

"What's up now?" asked John. "Where's the captain?"

"It is more of the work of the Black Star," cried Tomlinson, from the rear.

"We won't be in a hurry settling upon that," said David, hurriedly. "Now, Sam, man, what's the mischief?"

Sam came up quite out of breath, with his eyes as wild as those of a March hare.

In his fright he ran against a half-made trestle and upset it.

"Now, blunderbuss!" cried Ginger.

"He's dead," moaned Sam; "the captain's dead."

An exclamation of horror escaped those around.

They crowded about him, plying him with all sorts of eager questions, none of which he fairly grasped, and therefore did not answer.

"Stop, all of you!" cried John Trevelyn. "Give him time to get his breath. Now, Sam, pull yourself together, and tell us all about it."

"He would do it," groaned Sam.

"Do what?" cried Ginger, in a frenzy. "Why don't you speak out in a clear, perspikerous manner?"

" He would go down the cliff, and he fell," cried Sam.   " He's dead !"

" Take us to the spot," said David Trevelyn, " and let us really know the best and worst of the matter."

" Did you see him dead ?" asked John.

" I heard him fall," moaned Sam, " and when I spoke to him he didn't answer me."

" Come on, all of you," said David.   " Bring the ropes we've put together to haul the timber, also a few straight, strong spars.   Hurry up ! the captain's dead !   I, for one, will not believe it ; he wasn't born to die to-day or to-morrow."

The men hurriedly got the things required together, and at a trot, guided by Sam, they reached the spot where their leader had descended.

" He went over there," said Sam, pointing to the very place.

John Trevelyn stepped to the edge and peered over.

" There's a rock thirty feet below," he said, "but nothing on it."

" Then he's fallen into the water," said Sam, " and there's an end of him."

So all thought but the brothers Trevelyn, and they thought, as they usually did, in concert, that the fatal nature of the fall was not yet verified.

" Are you sure he went over there—at this very spot ?" asked David.

" Here are the marks made as he was getting over," replied Sam.

There, indeed, they were clear enough to the most inexperienced eye.

Nero too now came forward as a confirming witness.

After having looked over and sniffed the air he uttered the most dolorous howl ever emitted through the throat of a dog.

"The death cry," said Tomlinson, with a despairing gesture. "So they put their mark on me for *him*, and all this time I've been funking about myself. Why the deuce didn't they take me?"

"I wish they had," said Sam.

"It wouldn't 'a' mattered much to you all," continued Tomlinson, "for you'd still have had your leader. What will you do without him?"

It was a gloomy question enough, and the answer did not come readily.

It was Ginger who finally ventured to say—

"Well, we must do the best we can."

"Which certainly won't be much," muttered Tomlinson.

"Well, the captain isn't there," said David Trevelyn, "and if he's fallen off that rock and been drowned he is by this time down to the sea, and we shall never see him again."

"The tide may bring him back to the shore," replied Ginger; "it's on the turn."

There was that chance of seeing their young leader once again, and they all felt that it would be a mournful consolation to look upon him once more and make sure of his fate.

From where they stood they could not see the two caverns; nor were they visible to the eye at any point up and down that side of the river.

Thus they remained in ignorance of their existence, and in sad company wending their way to the beach.

There they waited the in-coming tide, and closely watched the waters for hours as they rolled in, but of course found not what they sought.

"I don't believe he's drowned," said Ginger, "if he was he was bound to have been brought in."

"Bar sharks," said Starbutt.

"Bar your jackass head!" said Ginger, politely.

"I don't believe any shark would have the audacity to touch him."

"Sharks ain't over bashful," muttered Tomlinson.

It was then late in the afternoon, and as it was useless to linger there any longer they returned to the place where they had been at work.

Half a hope, unuttered, was in the breasts of one and all that they would find their dear leader waiting them, but they were doomed to disappointment.

Nor did he come back to them that day.

Night succeeded day, and there was no indication whatever of his presence, nor anything beside Sam Gorgon's story to guide them to a true knowledge of his fate.

The mystery of it made it doubly, trebly, horrible, coming as it did as a climax to a series of startling events.

"The whole place is haunted," the seamen whispered to each other.

Gorgon and Sam were of the same opinion, and the brothers Trevelyn were troubled with doubts and fears upon the subject.

They drew apart, and sat in whispering consultation together, but nothing came of it.

"The watchword of his father must be ours," said David.

"Yes," replied John. "Watch and wait."

The watching and waiting of that day brought them nothing. The others slept and awoke to the fresh misery of another day.

A startling phenomenon presented itself to Herbert at the mouth of the cave.

CHAPTER XIV.

DISCOVERY OF THE CAPTAIN—A STRANGE EXPERI-
ENCE—GINGER TELLS HIS MEN WHAT OUGHT
TO BE DONE

"LET us hasten with the boat and get away," the men said.

Fear lent them strength, and they laboured like giants in getting down the timber, and sawing it into planks of the necessary length.

If they had for a moment believed that their captain was alive, and would be rescued they would never have thought of leaving the land until he was again with them.

But the tide of hopelessness had set steadily in. Not one believed they would ever see Herbert again.

Nero, the dog, was restless as they worked, wandering here and there, sniffing the air, and giving vent to howls that thrilled them through and through.

"Even the dog knows he's dead," said Tomlinson.

The men ate their meals as usual, for even the grief-stricken must eat to live, but Nero would touch nothing.

He would not so much as look at food. which the seamen regarded as an infallible sign that his master was dead.

They told stories with bated breath of dogs who had pined away when their masters were no more, scorning all food and refusing the caresses of those who offered to be their friends. Sam Gorgon was full of them, having picked them up when he travelled as a business man.

"We've lost him," said David Trevelyn, as the second night closed in.

"I fear so," responded John.

And with that conviction upon them they sought a much-needed rest.

All slept that night, and slept well, for despair and misery made them indifferent to foes and callous as to their fate.

They slept soundly too, and none awoke until the sun was shining on their faces.

On the rude rest they had made, lay the half-covered skeleton of the boat. One side was partly covered with planking, roughly cut but strong and serviceable. Another day and the boat would be ready for sea if they laboured as they had done before.

But lo ! the enemy had visited them during the night ; there was the fatal sign.

The ominous Black Star !

They did not cry out or indulge in gestures of terror when they beheld it, but got up and silently gathered around it.

"Why don't the devils show themselves?" asked David Trevelyn, in a paroxysm of fury. "Are they men, and have they the courage of men, and yet work only in the darkness ?"

"Watch and wait," said John, solemnly.

"I for one can't do it," replied his brother. "It is not a case for the exercise of patience, but for action. Let us wander about and cry aloud for them to come out of their hellish hiding place and face us."

"It would be another case of Glendower summoning spirits from the vasty deep," said John. "They will not come."

"They might," said Ginger, thoughtfully, smoothing his chin with his forefinger, "and I for one should like to have a cut at 'em."

All felt the impracticability of the proposition.

An enemy disposed for his own ends to hide, and also to do so with the certainty of not being found by their foes, would not answer such a summons.

" Let us finish the boat," said the men, "and to the deuce with the Black Star.

Then they looked around for their tools and found that all of any use had been taken away —the saws, the adzes, the hammers, the very nails.

A clean sweep had been made of everything.

This discovery roused them to a frenzy, and the men wandered up and down cursing their own carelessness and the cunning of the foe.

"Why did we all go to sleep?" they asked. "One at least might have watched."

None could hardly say how it was they had been so indifferent. The indifference had been that of half-drugged people, and they cried out that the very air had been poisoned to lull them into a feeling of indifference.

The brothers Trevelyn were especially cut to the quick about their own lack of watchfulness.

"We have been faithless to our trust," they said. "The captain bade us look after the rest if ill befell him, and we neglected our duty. The punishment falls upon us all."

But regrets were now worse than useless, and they set their heads together to devise some means of getting any. A raft was suggested, but how were they to cut down the timber for it?

If that could be done, the logs could be rolled down to the river and floated, but without the tools it was impossible.

One thing only could be done.

"We must leave this spot," said David, "and either march inland or along the shore."

The coast was rugged, and inland there was the semi-circle of mountains barring their way to a possibly better land.

The prospect was not cheering.

"Shall we pass another day here?" was the question put to the men ; and they one and all said "No."

"To wait here," they said, "is to be taken away one by one—who would care to be the last?"

The prospect of being in that position was terrible to all.

While they were in company some slight sense of security remained.

They had the arms they carried about them, and their little remaining store of provisions was untouched.

Go they must and would.

So the food that was left was divided and made into packages, which they bound upon their backs with all speed.

"Away," was now their watchword, and they prepared to set out.

The moment came when all were ready and the men started.

Nero, the dog, lying on the ground watched what was going on, and as the seamen starting first moved away John Trevelyn called to the dog to follow them.   But Nero did not stir.

Passively he regarded them, blinking his eyes and gently licking his lips with his tongue.

"Now, Nero," said John," "you have been a good dog, and we cannot leave you behind us. Up, boy, and with us."

But Nero did not attempt to rise.

He softly whined, and his head sinking down so as to rest upon his feet, he closed his eyes as if to sleep.

At a word from David Trevelyn the men halted and they all gathered round the dog.

"Come, Nero—good Nero," said John Trevelyn, patting him.

The dog blinked his eyes and stared about him in a semi-stupefied manner.

David stooped down and with his thumb raised one of the dog's eyelids.

"The poor beggar has been drugged," he said, "and that accounts for his not making any noise last night."

"Well! Sperrits don't go about drugging people and animals," said Ginger, looking about him with the air of an oracle, "and maybe arter all we've be been in too much of a funk over this business."

"But if not sperrits," asked Spifley, "who and what are they?"

"We'll find that out," said David. "Now, boys, don't let us give way, but just brace ourselves up to meet events."

"We can die but once," said Ginger.

"I've heard of a man as died twice," remarked Tomlinson.

"Oh! you did, and who may that be?" asked Ginger.

"He was hung—cut down and hung again," replied Tomlinson, meekly.

This explanation did not satisfy Ginger and he was proceeding to cross-examine his informant on the subject when David Trevelyn interposed.

"Now boys," he said, "you've got to decide what you will do—clear out—or have a good look round this part of the country first."

"We do as you do," the men said.

"Very well," replied David; "speaking for myself and my brother John," with whom by the way he had not recently exchanged a word on the subject, "we will do the latter."

They all agreed with them, the complete change in their movements being brought about by the discovery that Nero had been drugged by somebody ere the tricks of the previous night could be played upon them.

As the dog would not stir they decided to leave him there and go on a short journey of exploration, with the hope of falling in with some signs of the enemy.

Somehow all their hearts were the lighter for this alteration in the programme, and with a brisk step they set out towards the river.

"I vote we go and look again at the place where we left our captain," said Sam Gorgon.

"Agreed," said David Trevelyn, and towards that spot they bent their steps.

As they drew near it they closely examined the ground with the hope of finding some footmarks or trace of this mysterious enemy, but there were none.

Pursuing this occupation, none of them thought of looking across the river until they had reached the very verge of the cliff.

Then, as if by general consent, they looked across to the high land on the other side.

A general exclamation of alarm and surprise escaped them.

There, lying on his back, with his legs dangling over the cliff, was Herbert Standish, their gallant young leader. But whether alive or dead, it was impossible to say.

He lay so still that there was every probability of his being dead.

But how came he there?

On the previous day there had been no sign of him.

"He's been put there since last night," said Sam Gorgon.

"It seems to me," said David, drawing a deep breath, "that they've murdered him, and placed his body there so that we might see it."

"We've got to get to the other side and see if he's alive or dead," suggested John.

"Let us find a ford," said David, "or some place where we can swim across."

"I can't swim," said Sam.

So, said Starbutt and Spifley, and Ginger declared that "he was no great hand at it." So if all were to get over, some means of transit would have to be found.

They set out in search of it and or a mile up the stream the rapidly rushing water was dead against any of them getting over.

Then they came to a strange natural bridge, which gave them the means of transit they wanted.

It was a boring made by the river through a heap of rocks which had by some violent commotion of nature been thrust across the stream.

Tumbled together and wedged in they had no doubt for a brief time formed a barrier to the rushing stream.

But the under ones had been washed away and the upper ones, locked together remained to form a natural bridge.

It looked as if it were centuries old, for in the intersection of rocks plants and bushes, and, in a few places, trees were growing.

Altogether it was as strange a thing as they had ever seen in that strange land.

But something more immediately important than natural curiosities demanded their attention, and having scrambled over, they hastened to the spot where their leader was lying.

Nearly an hour had elapsed since they first saw him, but he had not changed his attitude.

"Dead," thought David, as he drew near him.

And so it seemed at first.

But when they had drawn him back from his dangerous position, John Trevelyn opened his garments, and laid a hand upon his heart.

"There is a faint pulsation," he said, "and he still lives."

This joyful news cheered them all, and the brothers Trevelyn undertook the task of restoring him.

Both had a knowledge of the plan of producing artificial respiration, and they treated Herbert precisely the same as they would have done if he had been rescued from drowning.

They worked his arms, chafed his limbs, and did many other things which those who care to read them will find in the printed instructions of the Royal Humane Society for such an emergency.

And they did not labour in vain.

Slowly the flame of life came back to their leader.

Opening his eyes he stared heavily about him, and it occurred to the lookers on that in the eyes he at that moment bore a strong resemblance to Nero as they had seen the dog that morning.

"Drugged, and by the same stuff!" exclaimed Ginger.

But why drug and not kill?

Therein lay yet another element of mystery.

He had evidently been completely in the power of someone, and it would have been an easy matter to dispose of him.

Why bring him here half dead, and leave him exposed in a place where there was so great a probability of his friends finding him?

These were the questions the lookers-on asked themselves, but they could not answer them.

Was Herbert able to do so?

It was some time ere he could speak, and when

he did, there was a curious harshness in his voice that told of much suffering and attendan weakness.

They asked him what had happened, and by degrees he told them the story of his adve itures to the point where he was left in this narrative.

"A ter a long silence," he went on, "which might have been of an hour's duration, or more or less, I cannot tell, I heard distinct sounds of a pick and hammer at work. Groping my way towards it I discovered that it came from the other side of my place of confinement. I worked my way round, and judged I was in a place about fifty feet in circumference."

"Was there a door?" asked David.

"No," replied Herbert, "nothing, as far as I could judge, but the solid, rugged rock."

"What was the floor like?"

"Perfectly smooth, as if of stone—but whether it was of that material I cannot tell."

"After that," he resumed, "I had another spell of silence which became almost unbearable. It was the most horrible thing I ever experienced. Then I heard a hiss, such as would emanate from a serpent. I judged it was one and prepared myself for an encounter with some sinewy denizen of the interior of the earth."

"Ugh!" exclaimed Sam Gorgon. "I should have fainted right away."

"It wouldn't have mattered what you did," said Ginger, loftily, "seeing as you wasn't there."

"I stood with my back to the rock," continued Herbert, "my arms extended, so as to grasp the reptile as it drew near, and, if possible, strangle it. But it came no nearer. But the hissing continued, and a peculiar aroma filled the place. Then I judged it was no living creature at all.

"I cannot describe to you my sensations as I

should like to do," said Herbert; "at first they were most delightful. I felt quite happy. Then ecstatic dreams came to me. I thought I was in a garden where the flowers were more magnificent than anything I had ever heard of or seen on earth. But my stay there was brief. Suddenly all changed. and I found myself fighting with fiends and all sorts of monsters, such as the morbid imagination of Virgil depicted. After that came oblivion, and I knew nothing more until I found myself here."

"The garden and the struggle were, of course, matters of fancy," said David

"Yes; the result of the action of some drug which I inhaled willingly, thanks to its seductive aroma; but who uses it I know no more than you do. I am glad I have gone through this experience."

"Glad?"

"Yes; it has given me the key to the fate of Richard Warden and my father. I can now understand how they were taken away without any disturbance. There is nothing supernatural in it."

"Carroll was over-drugged and died."

"That is why they left him," said Herbert; "and even in his death I find some consolation. It points to my father being yet alive."

"I hope he is," said Sam Gorgon, fervently.

"And Richard Warden, too," replied Herbert. "That they were taken away for a purpose—and not a good purpose—I really believe, but they were not murdered, and, with my experience, I have hopes of finding them alive."

"It seems strange that they did not keep you with them, sir," said Ginger.

"My good Ginger," said Herbert, "it is quite useless to speculate on that. Here I am, to my great satisfaction, and for the present that part must suffice. Here I will remain until I—"

He stopped short, for during the last few moments he had been mechanically feeling in the pocket of his tunic, from which he now drew a small square piece of the bark of some tree.

It was quite smooth on one side, but on the other was some writing, scratched by some sharp-pointed tool.

It was easily read, and ran as follows—

" Your life has been spared, but do not risk it more by remaining here. No good will come of it. You will not discover those who are lost. There is a path through the mountain in the north-east direction. You will have no difficulty in finding it. If in two days you or any of your people are found here your lives will be forfeited. Go, all of you, at once.   *"* BLACK STAR."

The writing was **very** close together, but being neatly written Herbert could read it right away.

This he did aloud to the great astonishment of his listeners.

" It is evident that one of our countrymen wrote this," said Herbert, " and I really see no reason why we should be afraid of him.

" You will not go," said David.

" Not until I know my father's fate."

" Well said—and we will remain with you."

" I just want to tackle one of them fumigating warmints," said Ginger. " I never had no great liking for any sort o' scent, which I consider a dollish thing and all wanity.

" And what would you do with him if you got hold on him, Mister Ginger ?" asked Starbutt.

" Make chips of him," replied Ginger, " and mind you this, all o' you men. When you gets the least aromatic effluvia coming round you, ust lay hold of your nose and have a hunt round for the fumigator. When you see him, go for him if he is as big as a house.

"Let us hope, Ginger," said David Trevelyn, "that if you are practised upon by our skulking enemy that you will be able to carry out your own instructions."

"There ain't no fear about me," returned Ginger, "for I've got a wonderful nose and can scent a thing out a mile off. They won't circumvent me."

Alas! for his being so cocksure. Ginger was destined to find out ere long that he was only mortal, with a nose no better than those possessed by his fellow men.

CHAPTER XV.

GINGER IS WITNESS OF A STRANGE SCENE—
THE DOG AND THE SAVAGE—A TERRIBLE
HURRICANE.

THE decision to remain was tempered with a resolution to be wary, and, if possible, deceive the foe.

Cunning should be met with cunning, until there was a chance of open warfare.

"If they can hide, so can we," said Herbert.

He was very weak, but rapidly getting better as the effect of the drug passed away.

Whatever it was it had the quality of relieving its victim when it evaporated, unless an overdose had been taken.

Herbert asked for his dog, and having been told of its condition, he wished to go back for it.

"Nero, like me," he said, "will get the better of it."

"It is too long a journey to go to-day," said David.

The day, indeed, was more than half spent, and Herbert was not as yet fit to journey far.

"I would gladly remain," he said, "if you think Nero will not go wandering away."

They could not see the spot where he had been left, but by going down the stream this was possible, at least so they thought and it was suggested by Ginger that somebody should do so.

The idea was not readily adopted for the general opinion was that the dog was safe—in addition, there was the prospect of a storm from the sea. Dark clouds were gathering and the wind was rising.

Ginger, not to be thwarted in an idea, went off alone, and speedily returned breathless, and in a state of glowing excitement.

"Nero's fighting with a man!" he gasped.

"What was he like?" asked Herbert.

"Could hardly tell," said Ginger, "they were rolling over and over, and rolled right out of sight behind some bushes as I was looking on. I judge the dog was getting the better of him."

In a moment all were upon their feet and moving in the direction Ginger had previously taken.

Herbert, considering his recent suffering, moved very quickly, and the brothers Trevelyn kept by his side.

The others went on a little way ahead.

Ginger, for the moment, was forgotten.

He, however, managed to follow them, but, being out of breath from recent exertion, could not quite keep up the necessary pace.

"Here—I say!" he gasped; "there's no immediate hurry."

But they paid no heed to him, simply because they did not hear him, and he, in disgust, pulled up.

"I'll wait here until you come back," he muttered, as he seated himself on a large stone.

We will leave him there and follow the rest, who gone some distance—about half a mile—ere the spot where Nero had been left, came into view.

Herbert, after the first spurt, had to slacken down his speed, and this made them longer in getting there than they otherwise would have been.

And when they did get into a position to view the spot, they saw that Ginger had not been mistaken or romancing.

The dog and man were in sight—the man lying straight and still upon the ground, the dog in a crouching position with his paws on the man's breast.

"Why, that's the savage we saw on the log!" exclaimed Sam Gorgon.

"And the dog's killed him," said David Trevelyn.

"He don't look like a dead man to me," replied Herbert. "I have good eyes, and I see no signs of his being wounded. I should say, rather, that he is shamming death, or simply keeping still. A dog will seldom worry a quiet man."

"Off again!" shouted the three seamen together.

The savage had suddenly jumped to his feet, and with incredible swiftness on the part of a man made a dash for the river.

Nero bounded after him; but the good dog had not yet quite recovered from the effect of the drug, and he ran comparatively slow.

It was a level race between the man and dog right down to the river, into which the savage plunged head first and disappeared.

Nero boldly followed, but the moment the good dog leaped into the water he was carried at a great rate towards the sea.

Nero was borne away alone, battling for his canine existence.

No help could be given him, and it was quite useless to give him an encouraging word, as he was about as helpless as a straw on the surface of that swiftly coursing stream.

They watched him until he was a mere speck in the distance, and then he was finally lost in the haze of the advancing storm.

"It seems to me, sir," said Tomlinson, "that a regular hurricane is coming from the sea. Heaven help any ship that is near the land."

"In five minutes it will be upon us," said David Trevelyn, "we ought to seek some sort of refuge. Look yonder at the trees, bending like reeds before it."

There was, indeed, no time to dally, and they all ran for the shelter of a high rock on the bank of the river.

Not until then had the absence of Ginger been observed.

"Where's Mr. Ginger?" said Starbutt, as they settled into their places behind the rugged shelter.

"Well, I'm blessed," exclaimed Tomlinson, "if there isn't another gone."

"He was pumped out," said John Trevelyn, "and of course could not keep up with us. He will see the storm and take care of himself."

Ginger had to take care of himself for nobody there could help him, and a few moments later the storm burst.

It was as anticipated, a hurricane, and the worst that had ever come under the experience of those who witnessed it.

The wind swooped down upon the land like a roaring monster, driving everything before it.

Uprooted trees went flying by like leaves, and

With his legs dangling over the cliff their gallant leader hung.

the very rock that sheltered the party quivered to its base.

The rain fell as it seemed in masses from the clouds, striking the earth in a slanting direction.

Where the soil was soft great holes were washed in it and filled with water, only to be emptied in a few moments by the driving wind.

There was lightning and thunder too.

The latter could not be clearly distinguished from the roaring of the storm, but the latter was blinding and bewildering.

It zig-zagged in every direction in the sky, darting down and striking the earth.

Trees stripped of their branches, but whose trunks defied the wind, were struck by the withering fluid, the bark ripped up and tossed in among the chaos of rubbish that was whirling in every direction.

It seemed scarcely possible that anything movable by any elemental force would escape the all-powerful storm.

Sheltered as they were, the crouching men had to remove their hats and cling together to prevent themselves being torn out of their hiding-place and carried away.

Poor Ginger!

They thought of him in their trouble, and gave him up for lost.

Unless he had secured a safe hiding-place there was literally no chance of his escaping with life.

It was brief if it was terrible.

Half an hour at the outside sufficed for it to spend its fury on that district.

The huge black clouds went rolling by, rolling up, it appeared, like mountains before the power of the wind, and they saw the rain, like a wall of water, sweep on ahead to the mountain district, where, for a time, it blotted out everything.

Then the sun shone out and the wind sank down
to a ordinary gale.

That could be faced, and they crept out to look
upon such a scene of destruction as the eye of man
has seldom dwelt upon.

Of all the great trees which had stood proudly
erect only a few were left standing.

And they had been stripped of nearly all their
foliage, leaving them uncanny, weird-like specimens
of the class.

All around was as desolate as a blasted heath.

The hand of death laid upon a place could not
have left it more desolate.

The sea, though some distance away, thundered
in the shore so that it could be heard plainly by
them.

It sounded like some huge cataract close by.

To the river they hurried and saw that its waters,
risen many feet, were one mass of foam, mingled
with the trunks of trees, twisting and turning in
the eddying waters.

The seamen, accustomed to many a wild evolution
of the elements, were awe-stricken.

They had never seen—never heard of the like
of this.

CHAPTER XVI.

MARVELLOUS RE-APPEARANCE OF GINGER —
IRQUOI, THE STRANGE SAVAGE—THE TWO
MESSAGES.

"POOR Nero !" was Herbert's first exclamation.

It did not seem at all probable that the gallant
dog could have survived the storm.   As for Ginger,
they gave him up for lost.

But as in duty bound they wended their way
back to look for him.

To find the spot where they parted from the old

boatswain was not at all an easy matter, everything around them was so changed.

Only the sturdier rocks remained in their places.

The smaller ones had been rolled here and there, and masses of small stones lay scattered far and wide.

Their only guide was the cliff-like banks of the river, and even there the destroying hand had been at work.

The ledge on which Herbert fell had been torn from its support and had disappeared in the bed of the river.

The two caves were exposed to the daylight.

Into the one which had received a portion of the river, a body of water was rushing in, filling up almost the whole of the cavity.

The landing stage, as we called it, of the next cave was under water.

Wreck and ruin everywhere.

Poor Ginger !

They walked on, looking for him, without a hope of seeing the old salt any more alive.

Newly-made hollows in the earth were examined with the hope of finding him. They peered under overturned rocks, and examined the heaps of trees which had become locked together.

But there was no Ginger.

They called for him separately, and in concert ; but the only answer was the echo of their own voices.

" He's gone !" said Standish. " Moved clean away to the mountains."

"As a sample of storms," remarked Sam Gorgon, "this was about the neatest thing I ever heard of. I hope they don't come this way often."

"Not likely," said John Trevelyn, "or how could these trees have grown to the size they are. Some of them are a century old."

It was evident that the storm was phenomenal even in these parts.

Ahead it looked like a huge wall of black marble rising from the ground to the sky.   It was awe-inspiring, terrorising.

Suddenly an exclamation escaped Tomlinson.

"Here's Mister Ginger's hat," he said.

There it was lying, pretty well smashed, with the trunk of a fallen tree resting upon it.

His hat being there Ginger could not be far away.

"Poor Ginger!" sighed Sam Gorgon, as he scooped a tear out of his eye.   "He wasn't a bad sort of fellow all round."

"He was a man of some larning," said Tomlinson, "and he made the most on it."

They were all sorry for Ginger, and not a little anxious about themselves.   It seemed more than ever as if they were doomed to be thinned out one by one, and each, as before, thought of himself as the last man.

That Ginger had not been killed in the ordinary way during the storm was clear, for all their searching produced nothing but his smashed hat, which the seamen reserved to keep as a relic of the "old 'un," as they somewhat irreverently called the boatswain.

On Herbert rested a feeling of keen dissatisfaction

He was angered against his unseen foe, and his resolve not to yield to any form of pressure put upon him was stronger than ever.

He could not go away until he knew something more of the fate of his friends.

But at the same time he would meet stratagem with stratagem, subterfuge with subterfuge.

"We will sham leaving this spot," he said, "and take the direction pointed out to us in that letter."

It was evening before they started, and they walked through a land smitten by the storm in a manner inconceivable save by those who witnessed it, and halted not until darkness set in.

They bivouacked in a rugged patch of country, a silent, thoughtful band.

During the night the seamen took turns at watching, but neither saw nor heard anything to report.

Early in the morning Herbert examined the ground around him, and discovered distinct traces of a trail, which he had not noted in the dusk of the evening before.

It led back to the river in one direction, and in the other it bore away to the mountains.

He had, therefore, been led by chance to take a road with which somebody was very familiar.

Leaving the men preparing breakfast with such scanty means as they had, Herbert sauntered a little way along the trail, taking the backward route.

Sam Gorgon accompanied him, and they both carried a rifle with the hope of getting something to shoot at which would add to their small stock of food.

Ere they had gone far a small deer leaped up from behind a pile of stones and dashed across their path.

Herbert's quick eye saw it's first movement, and he brought it down before it could get twenty yards away.

"This will be welcome," he said to Sam. "Go back and ask Tomlinson or one of the others to come and skin it."

Sam turned to obey, but he had no need to go. The shot had been heard, and the others in a body were running up to see what was the matter.

They were overjoyed to find it was an addition to their miserable larder, and the seamen, shouldering the dead deer, carried it back to their camp, where they had lighted a fire.

The brothers Trevelyn accompanied them, and Herbert and Sam slowly sauntered in the rear, gradually falling behind.

Suddenly they were startled by a gasping sound behind them, and turning they beheld a spectacle that fairly took their breath away. It was so astounding.

There was the lost Ginger staggering along with a savage in his arms, holding him in an iron grip from which few men could have escaped.

Nay, more, it was *the* savage—the swarthy creature who had been seen on the floating log and fighting with Nero, the dog.

He was struggling for his liberty; but the iron arms of Ginger held him tight.

Herbert cocked his rifle as they drew near, and fixed his eye sternly on the savage, who certainly understood the look and action, as he immediately became passive.

"I've got him!" gasped Ginger. "It was that hot o' yourn as give me the chance. I heerd and he heerd it, and as he turned to see what it was I grabbed him."

"Put him down," said Herbert. "He comprehends *me*. Does he speak English?"

"I don't know, sir," replied Ginger, as he put the savage on his feet and proceeded to wipe his perspiring brow, "for niver a word has he said to me yet."

"You shall tell me all about this strange affair by-and-bye," said Herbert. "Be assured that we are glad to see you are still alive."

Sam Gorgon, who had been in a speechless state of astonishment up to that moment stepped forward and grasped Ginger by the hand.

"Marvellous!" was all he said.

"So you would say," replied Ginger, "if you knowed all. But, there, I'll tell you about it later on."

Herbert and the savage stood face to face, eyeing each other.

You have all heard or read of the power of the eye of a brave man over a wild beast.

If a man can look a lion or tiger full in the face *without the least shrinking* he will subdue that beast; but let him quail in the slightest and he is lost.

Now it was something of a similar nature between Herbert and this savage.

If our hero had shrunk in the least from the gaze of the other he would have had either to shoot the man or let him go.

But the eyes of the savage though fierce enough at first, gradually sank beneath Herbert's fixed gaze until they rested on the ground.

He was—for the time, at least—subdued.

"Who are you ?" demanded Herbert.

Not a movement of the lip or the least sound was offered by way of reply.

"You understand me, I can see," said Herbert, coolly. "I give you three seconds to answer me. One !"

There was just the least possible quivering of the eyelids of the savage.

"Two !"

A shrinking back and a quick glance to the right, as if looking for some way of escape.

"Th—"

The rifle was levelled, and Herbert's finger was on the trigger.

The savage, with a wild cry, threw himself at his feet.

"Mercy !" he gasped.

"Rise," said Herbert, "and answer a few

questions I may put to you ; you will then receive no harm."

"No fraid," said the savage, slowly rising.

It was an assertion that made Sam Gorgon laugh ; but the bearing of the savage was not that of a coward.

He turned his full dark eyes on Sam with a look that dried up the fun of our friend.

"No fraid," he said again. "Die—well ; but not so."

He laid his hand upon the rifle as he spoke, making his meaning clear.

It was that particular form of death he dreaded.

"Again," said Herbert, "who are you ?"

"Irquoi," he answered.

"What are you ?" asked Herbert.

"King right hand," replied the savage, proudly. "Go here—all place—do all tings."

"And who is your king ?"

A fixed look came into the savage's face, and once more he was dumb.

"You have to tell me," replied Herbert. "First, tell me how it is you speak English ?"

"Englishman tell me," replied Irquoi. "Talk king—talk all. No say more. Kill !"

He threw up his arms as he spoke, and with an indescribable look of proud defiance prepared to meet the doom he evidently most dreaded.

He had said who he was, but he would not reveal the secrets of his master.

This fidelity won the heart of Herbert. How could he kill one so brave and true ; and of what good service to him would be the death of the man ?

"Irquoi," he said, "I will not kill you."

"No kill ?" exclaimed Irquoi, in calm surprise.

"No. Go back to your king or your master," said Herbert, "and tell him that I wish to see him face to face, to call him to account for the wrongs he has done to me and mine. Do you understand me?"

Irquoi's face bore a puzzled look, but it did not arise from his want of comprehension.

"King no wrong," he said; "king all right."

"How can he be?" asked Herbert. "Has he not robbed me of a friend—of my father? Have I not seen one that he slew?"

Irquoi shook his head.

"No king do it," he said.

"Who, then, did these these things?" demanded Herbert.

"White men?" Irquoi answered.

"Where can I find these men?" asked our hero.

"No tell, unless king say so," returned Irquoi.

"Go back to your king and say I would see him. I will not leave this place until you return."

"No kill king, no kill anyone, if come?" inquired Irquoi.

"No," said Herbert. "We did not come here to harm anyone. As for the white men you speak of, will you take a message to them?"

Irquoi nodded.

"Tell them that they are cowardly skulkers," said Herbert. "Repeat the words."

Irquoi repeated the words thrice, and then said he would not forget."

"Ask them to come out from their den and face us," continued Herbert, "and man for man we will give a good account of ourselves."

Irquoi's eyes lighted up. The message pleased him. It was evidently in harmony with the spirit within him.

Herbert would fain have detained him a little longer to ask him more questions, but he was impatient to bring things to a head. He felt that he had at last broken open the door of the mystery, and ere long would be acquainted with all behind it.

One word more he had with him.

"Irquoi," he said, "I am your friend—friend—you understand? Come to me when you please, and I will not harm you. Now go and take my message to your king and to those white skulkers, who, I feel sure, are at the bottom of all the mischief."

Irquoi drew back a pace ; then, with a sweeping motion, bowed to the very ground. The next moment he was flying back like a deer in the direction of the river.

CHAPTER XVII.

GINGER'S NARRATIVE — TUALCAMACHI, THE SAVAGE KING—THE STORY OF HIS WRONGS AND WOES.

GINGER had to tell the story of his adventures, and in its way it was a remarkable narrative.

Shortly after he fell behind his friends he found himself out of breath, and sat down to rest.

A few moments later he heard a rustling sound behind him, but did not take much notice of it.

"It warn't a noise to bother a man," he said ; "but I was thinking over what it was like when about as curious a smell as ever I knowed came up to my nose."

"And you laid hold o' your nose, in course ?" said Tomlinson.

"I did not," replied Ginger, "although I intended to do so later on. It was an aromatic hodour—a sort o' herbs and chemicals mixed up, and I gave two good sniffs at it, and then—"

Ginger stopped short and looked about him in

a somewhat foolish manner.   Apparently he had come to a deadlock in his yarn.

" And then?" suggested David Trevlyn.

" Why then," said Ginger, " I didn't sniff any more."

" Why not ?"

" I went right orf, and didn't remember no more until this morning, when I found myself over yonder, about half a mile from here, lying in a hole—a kind o' cave—with that nigger chap sitting by me."

" I was a thinking what I'd do to him," continued Ginger, " when we heard the capen's rifle, and Mister Nigger looking round, I up and seizes him round the waist, and brings him along, just as you see me a-doing."

" Then you didn't hear anything of the storm ?" asked Herbert.

" Storm !" said Ginger.   " Has there been a storm ?"

Then they told him of the hurricane, and he listened amazed ; and he was more astonished still when he heard how far he had been carried by the savage Irquoi.

The inference was that while endeavouring to carry Ginger away the savage was overtaken by the storm, and with his charge fairly *blown* part of the way.

This idea received some confirmation in the discovery made by Ginger, that he had some very extensive bruises in the most prominent parts of his body.

" They ain't things as I takes much count on as a rule," he said, " but here they are, and I reckon by the size of 'em that I must have been trundled along like a ball, and, what is more, that savage chap must ha' stuck to me.   *He's* as hard as nails ; he felt like an iron man in my arms."

The missing links of Ginger's story remained a matter of surmise for the time, and the next speculation was as to the personality and nature of the " king " of whom Irquoi had spoken.

And would he come; or was he held in semi-captivity by the men who were at least English as far as their tongue was concerned ?

To Herbert the main question bore upon his father's fate.

Was he alive ?

The probability of his life having been spared had materially increased in strength, but the reason of his captivity was as much of a mystery as ever.

"Once more my father's motto must be adopted," said Herbert, to himself. " Watch and wait."

The king did not arrive that day or the next, and the time hung terribly on their hands.

They cut up the deer, and dried the flesh, as the trappers of America used to do, each man being apportioned his share.

Another night passed, and the day came again.

Herbert and the brothers Trevelyn climbed up an adjacent hill and carefully scanned the country round. A few deer browsing in the distance were all they could see of life.

"Irquoi has not succeeded in inducing his majesty to come out of his retreat," said John Trevelyn, grimly.

Herbert did not answer him, but his brow looked dark. He was getting tired of the delay, and felt as if he would like to rip the earth open and lay bare the secret of the caverns which were undoubtedly the hiding-place of his foes.

Walking ahead he descended the hill, and slowly wended his way back to the camp.

Their path lay beside a babbling little stream, which lower down ran into the turbid river. The banks were rough and they had to pick their way through strange shaped rocks and stones.

Half the distance or thereabouts had been accomplished when an exclamation from David caused Herbert to look up.

Before him stood two savages, Irquoi and another many years older.

The latter was far advanced in life, with a fine head of white hair and a flowing beard. His apparel was as simple as that of his servitor.

With great composure he stood still, and Irquoi came forward and bowed low.

"My king," he said—" Tualcamachi—great and good."

Herbert doffed his hat to the king, who responded with a gentle inclination of his head.

Then he advanced a few paces slowly, and Herbert advanced with outstretched hand.

This sign of friendship Tualcamachi was familiar with, for he stretched out his own hand and eagerly grasped the one extended towards him.

His eyes, keen and dark rested on Herbert's rifle, and an eager look sprang into his face.

"No kill?" he said.

"No kill," repeated Herbert, " no harm to you. I am your friend, unless—

He stopped short, and a spasm of pain passed over his face.

"You took two of my friends away," he said. "Where are they?"

"No take any," eagerly replied Tualcamachi; "no harm white man."

"Let us go to my camp," said Herbert; "we can sit there and talk. You may trust me. Here, take this."

He extended his rifle towards the savage king, whose face expressed a variety of emotions that did not find expression in words.

But he took the rifle and examined it with a delighted face. He patted and hugged it to his heart as if it had been a child."

"Me kill now," he said; "but not you, friend—kill dem.'

He swept his hand towards the spot where Herbert had met with his strange adventures in the cave, and a positively malevolent light gleamed in his eyes.

"Kill dem—kill dem," he muttered, as he walked by Herbert's side.

"How many are there?" asked Herbert, as they moved slowly along.

The king held up a hand with the fingers extended, closed them once, extended them again, and then held up two.

"Twelve," said Herbert, "and there are eight of us. The odds are not very great."

He did not talk any more to the old savage, who, as they walked along occupied his time in fondling and examining the deadly weapon he carried.

Close behind Irquoi stalked, grave and silent.

David and his brother John brought up the rear with their rifles cocked and ready to avenge any attempt at treachery.

But Tualcamachi meant none.

Herbert was to him a friend, and perhaps something more, for his bearing towards him bordered on the reverential.

They reached the camp when the others were lying about at rest. They all sprang to their feet on seeing the strange savages.

Ginger, who was occupied in trying to get his battered hat into shape again, hailed Irquoi as an old friend.

"What cheer, messmate?" he said.

Irquoi smiled, and it was the first time they had

seen him do so, exhibiting two rows of strong, white teeth; "sample grinders," as Sam Gorgon called them.

"Draw a little aside," said Herbert to his followers, " I must have a talk with the king.

They drew aside, and Irquoi remained with his chief, over whom he watched with the devotion of a son.

When the old king sat down upon the ground beside Herbert, he reclined at his feet like a watchdog.

"Tualcamachi," said Herbert, "what of my friends, are they all alone?"

"Alone," was the answer.

"Why did you not bring them with you?"

"Me no have then," said the Savage King. "White man shut up all dark—make work—dig —dig—"

"Show us where they are," said Hubert, springing to his feet.

"No go yet—wait," said Tualcamachi; "go slow—creep—creep— go at dem—Tualcamachi— not miss.   He go worship great star—go for two days."

A cunning look passed over the face of the savage, and something like a chuckle was heard from the lips of Irquoi.

"No let me come out," continued Tualcamachi, "but worship star in cave—through hole—top— I know way out."

This time the king and his subject chuckled together; they had evidently humbugged somebody and were making merry over it.

"Tell me about those men," said Herbert, "and how you came together."

Tualcamachi became suddenly very grave.

Rising to his feet he took up a dignified attitude and began his story.

There was the lost Ginger staggering along with a savage in his arms.

"Long go—many moons" (he opened and shut his hands several times very rapidly), "Tualcamachi, king of many people" (again there was the expressive motion of the fingers), "live happy—worship star—got men—live in great cave—all right—no tears—no groans.

"He get herb—make good ting to sleep," he went on. "All well—one day—come white man —many—bring boat—shoot—fire. Tualcamachi go with people—say—welcome—give meat—fruit —herb. White man take all—den shoot—kill."

He uttered the last few words with a wail in which Irquoi joined.

"People not kill run away," he resumed, indicating with his hand that they fled to the mountains, "Tualcamachi felt heavy shot here," he touched his side, "Irquoi too—both take— white man cruel—beat both—make starve. King has to cook—wash. Irquoi—hunt—but not go far—or white man kill king. White man go to cave—dig—dig—find nothing—all dig—watch for oder white men—come—you—oders—dey go— take me, too—give good sleep stuff—carry way— give one too *much*—he die—so leave him."

Disjointed as his story was, he let in sufficient light to guide Herbert to the main facts of his story.

Tualcamachi lived when at peace with a small tribe of people.

One day white men with arms, to which he was an utter stranger, came there and proceeded first to slaughter his people, then made him captive, and, finally, went digging in the strange caves which had been the home of the savage monarch.

But digging for what?

That was a mystery; but Herbert cared not if it never were solved.

His first thought and care was to rescue his

father and Richard Warden, whom he now knew to be alive and in captivity.

Slaves to the body of twelve men who had come thither on some strange quest.

From Irquoi he learnt two things.

First, that the only idea of a boat in their minds was a log upon the stream, and that they had ancient flint instruments with which they could cut down a tree and trim it to the size required.

It must have been dreadfully slow work; but it was done and many had been used by the tribes in the upper waters of the river in the old days.

He had been out hunting on the day when Herbert and Sam Gorgon saw him, and finding one of the old logs lying wedged in the shore he put it afloat and returned to the cave.

It was nothing new in the way of feats.

He and others used in the old days to carry their wood down to the cave by that route.

By getting into a certain current they would make sure of being carried into the cave and landing in one of its inner parts, of which we shall hear more anon.

It seemed also that the white men had inspired both the king and his followers with a mortal terror of firearms, and had humbugged them into a belief that they would go on " speaking death " for ever.

But who the white men were, and what was the object of their continual " dig—dig," Tualcamachi did not know.

" You must take me there to-night," said Herbert; " all of us. We are strong, we do not fear, and our guns are better than theirs."

" But no kill," said Tualcamachi, gently; " only send sleep. Good herb—strong smell— much sleep."

" Well, we shall see," said Herbert.

CHAPTER XVIII.

THE MIDNIGHT JOURNEY TO THE CAVE—A SURPRISE.

RQUOI and Tualcamachi held a long conference together in low tones, apart from everyone else, and it was plain that the king was troubled.

The cause of it was soon after made clear by Irquoi.

He came over to Herbert, and in his broken English told him that there must be no lives taken in the cave.

"No fight if you help," he said.

"I have always said that I will avoid it, if possible," replied Herbert; "it all depends on the men I have to deal with. What I principally want is my father back again."

Irquoi conveyed these words back to the king, who was a little easier; but for some reason he was not quite satisfied.

However, nothing more was said to Herbert on that score, and preparations were begun to invade the cave at night, not by the way that Herbert entered it before, but by another inland.

He learnt that the cave was of great extent, branching off in various directions, with many passages and halls, some of which Irquoi told him were the homes of the stars.

Tualcamachi and his people were star worshippers, and from these, the men working in the cave, had adopted the sign.

As for the paint used, the savage told our hero

that it was found in its natural state in many places on the island, and given its indelible qualities by the action of boiling.

The peculiar aroma by which many of our friends had been reduced to senselessness was prepared only by Irquoi, who, in his way, was a medicine man to the king.

The strangers had been allowed the use of it, but the secret of its manufacture was kept from them.

They were very anxious to obtain it, for it would be an invaluable thing to take home with them when they left.

And means of getting it away seemed even at their command, for Irquoi spoke of a strange, big boat lying off the island in the direction of the mountains secured by a coral reef that rose above the sea from the action of storms.

Now one thing was clear to Herbert, and that was the coming of these men was not accidental.

For a certain purpose they had come to the island, and up to the present that purpose had not been accomplished.

Perhaps they were not so murderous a band as the attack upon the natives led him at first to believe, for they had spared the lives of his father and Richard Warden, and the death of Carroll seemed to be quite an accidental matter.

Altogether things were very puzzling, and he could only await the issue of his night's quest with the hope of solving everything.

Irquoi had some idea of our mode of calculating time, having probably seen a watch in the possession of the strangers, for he spoke of its taking "two hours" to reach the inland entrance to the caves.

It was dark that night about eight o'clock, and by that time all arrangements were made.

Everything in the way of superfluous stores, which was not much, was hidden away, and they set out.

Irquoi, Tualcamachi, and Herbert led, the brothers Trevelyn brought up the rear.

The first-named was the real guide, and he bore away through a part of the country hitherto untrodden by our friends.

The trail lay through ground that was rough in places, and by-and-bye they came to a group of small hills, packed close together in a circular form. In the centre of these the savage told Herbert the strangers camped.

It was for the time being their home.

And there also was the way into the caves which they must seek.

Irquoi guided the party, who was now instructed to maintain a strict silence, between two of the hills by a very narrow path.

The way was fairly lighted by the brilliant stars and a young moon, so that obstacles over which in darkness they might have stumbled could be clearly seen.

The open space was at hand, and Irquoi, signalling to the others to be silent, went on alone to reconnoitre.

Tualcamachi squatted on the ground, with his head bent low, his body rocking slowly to and fro.

The old man was again perturbed.

Neither he nor his people had ever been fighting men, and the prospect of war troubled him.

A quarter of an hour elapsed, and then Irquoi came swiftly gliding back again.

"All gone," he said ; "all work."

This was an intimation that the camp was deserted, and with their guide a few paces in front of them they hastened on.

In a few minutes they emerged into the open space between the hills.

It was about two hundred yards across, shut in for the most part—a very secluded spot.

Rude shelters for sleeping had been put up here and there, and in the centre a fire was burning.

Suspended on a tripod of poles was a huge iron pot, from which arose a savoury odour.

The supper of the men was there, simmering but untended.

A few paces to the left was the entrance of the cavern, an opening about five feet wide and six high, and into it Irquoi, the king, and Herbert hastened.

The others followed a few paces behind, each man with his weapon ready for use if occasion should arise.

It was a time for excitement with them all, but there was no sign of hesitation or anything approaching fear, for the clouds of superstition were dispelled.

They knew that with men alone they had to deal, and the fact of their being more numerous was of small account.

On down a dark way, with a smooth, sandy floor, they went, until a faint shimmering ahead warned them that they were approaching the men they sought.

A turn in the cave brought Herbert into full view of three men engaged with pick and axe digging.

Two lanterns were suspended from the roof, which

was rather low, showing that two-thirds of the cavern in view had been worked upon.

Only three.   Then where were the other nine?

Herbert did not wait to find that out, but stood forward, and in a quiet, determined tone, said—

"Stand, all of you.   Move not for your lives!"

The startled men, who had the appearance of men of the mining class, stood quite still, staring at him with unconcealed dismay.

"Disarm yourselves," said Herbert, with rifle ready; "lay down even your tools and give yourselves up."

"Wall," said the foremost, with an unmistakable American accent, "I call this somewhat sudden. Pards, we've got to cave in."

He threw down his pick, and drawing a pair of pistols from his pockets laid them on the heap of dirt before him.

The others did the same, and they all stood quiet enough, waiting to see what was coming next.

"Ginger," said Herbert, "you know how to secure their arms—do it."

Ginger had some pieces of rope handy, these being part of the preparations for the evening, and with a few expert turns and a knot or two secured their arms.

While the operation was being performed they looked at each other in a very stupid manner.

"I reckon," said the man who had spoken before "that this is about as sudden as it could be.   It's like a new style of star worshipping, old Leatherhead, isn't it?"

Tualcamachi whom he addressed, received this remark with dignified indifference, but Irquoi's eyes flashed, and he made a movement as if he would have gone for the speaker, but a look from Herbert restrained him.

So far the night expedition had been successful ; but the great object of their coming had yet to be attained.

"You have some prisoners here," said Herbert.

The man laughed and looked at his comrades, who grinned.

"I am not disposed to treat it as a jest," said Herbert. "Where are they ?"

"Down in the white caves," was the answer, "a-working with our other pards."

"Where are the White Caves ?"

"On ahead, mister—for a half mile or so. The blessed land here is honey-combed with 'em. The Kentucky Mammoth Cave is a fool to it, and I've seen *that*."

"You must show us the way," said Herbert.

"No, I'll be darned if I do !" said the other. "My name's Sprague, and I'm a true pard—I'll die afore I'll sell my pals !"

"Hear, hear !" said the others.

"Hear me," said Herbert. "All I want is my father and his friend. They are alive, you tell me ?"

"Sure they are," said Sprague. "We don't want to shed the blood o' white men over this job. At the same time, we don't want any interference."

"Whatever your object may be," said Herbert, "is nothing to me. Give me back my father and friend and I'll ask no more."

"And when you've got em' what will you do ?" asked Sprague, with a leer.

"Leave the place, if we can ; but it seems to be somewhat difficult to do so."

"It's a derned enchanted place, that it is," said Sprague, with a grin. "All hobgoblins and sich like. Whoop, there!"

He turned his face to the inside of the cave and uttered this shout just as the sound of approaching footsteps and voices fell upon their ears.

The footsteps were hurried, and the voices calling on somebody to stop.

"Whoop, there! Ware hawks!" shouted Sprague.

"Silence for your life!" said Herbert, thrusting him back. "Silence all!"

A significant touch upon the barrel of his weapon by Herbert sufficed for the prisoners.

They were all brave men enough, but they were not so foolish as to risk their lives needlessly.

The voices ahead increased, and the echoes in the cave multiplied them by ten. Judging by sound alone, quite a host of noisy people appeared to be approaching.

Herbert and his followers stood with their weapons at the ready, prepared for immediate use if necessary, and in a few moments two men appeared at a turn in the cave.

They were running fast, and both were hatless and unarmed.

Even in the gloom Herbert recognised the beloved form of his father, and with a wild cry of delight rushed forward to meet him.

But James Standish for the moment did not recognise his son.

"Get out of my way!" he shouted, hoarsely. "I've had enough of this devil's home and will not be taken alive.

"Father, don't you know me?

"Herbert, my son!"

They fell into each other's arms, forgetful for the moment of all else but the joy of the re-union.

Richard Warden, the second man, recalled them to their position by crying out—

"Here they come. We've got to fight—and, good Heaven! we've got them in front and behind us."

"Friends behind us," cried Herbert. "Father, stand beside me. I am strong enough now to fight a host."

Quite a little host was indeed approaching— armed, furious men, who came dashing forward until they espied Herbert and his friends.

The latter had now drawn up close to their leader, dragging their prisoners with them.

Weapons were in readiness for the promised encounter.

"Let me speak to 'em," said Sprague. "I don't want any bloodshed, and I'm pretty well certain you don't. But once it begins it's extarmination from one side or the other."

"Speak out then, quick," said Herbert.

"Pards," shouted Sprague, "there's no call for a row. These ere gentlemen want nothing but the two people *who've been staying with us.*"

"Hang you for an impudent scoundrel!" said James Standish; "staying with you! Herbert, you can't trust these men. My life and Warden's were spared because of some childish superstition they had got about shedding white men's blood. Up with your hands there, all of you."

Quick as light almost, he snatched two re- volvers from the hands of one of the sailors and presented them at the knot of men in front.

These weapons had recently been taken from Sprague and his two companions.

"Cut !" shrieked Sprague.

It was a short way of telling the men to run, and in a moment as it seemed, they had vanished.

James Standish fired two shots into the gloom, but there was no indication of their having taken any effect.

"Now," said Sprague, coolly, "you'd better get over your job with us as quickly as possible, for I don't like to be kept waiting for *anything*."

"What do you mean ?" demanded Herbert.

"Why, the hanging," said Sprague. "Of course, you'll put us up on the nearest tree. If you were in my place and I in yours you'd hang as sure as eggs is eggs."

CHAPTER XIX.

A FEW NEEDED EXPLANATIONS—THE HOME OF THE GREAT STAR.

"DON'T imagine your fate is in my hands," Herbert said, "I leave you to my father and Richard Warden. It is they whom you have wronged. They shall be your judges."

To follow the men who had lately beat a retreat was not advisable, and Irquoi said—

"Much cave—no find—but stop hole and keep

in," which was, in a concise way, a picture of the situation and a plan for the future treatment of the men.

Enough had been done for the night. Herbert's heart was light, and all round the joy was general.

Taking their prisoners with them they returned to camp for the night.

Then it was that Irquoi came out with an astounding piece of information.

"Close cave," he said; "no get out out this way."

He called Herbert's attention to the position of an upright and apparently fixed piece of rock on the right hand side of the cave.

"Push—one—two men," he said.

Ginger lent him a hand, laughing at the idea of such a huge rock being shifted by two men; but move it did, and glided like a sliding door across the mouth of the cave, closing it up.

It seemed to travel on something round beneath it, balls or rollers.

Nobody there was more astonished than Sprague.

"Dern you!" he said, to Tualcamachi, "that's one thing you kept from us."

His majesty, as before, favoured him with no reply, but Irquoi cut a defiant, derisive caper before him.

"You see someting," he said, "but not much. You dig—dig—find noting—but me know—and me show friend Herbert. Yah! yosh! So—you —FOOL!"

The exasperation of Sprague was evident.

Here was a man whom he had hitherto treated as a slave laughing at him, and declaring that he knew the secret of the hiding-place of *something*, for which he and his comrades had long searched in vain.

What was that something?

Herbert asked Irquoi, and the savage laughed, showing two rows of white teeth that would have excited the envy of a professional beauty.

"Me show you, by-bye."

With this Herbert was content, but Sprague was not. He was in a terribly heated state, as he sat with his dejected comrades, arms still secured, and watched over by Starbutt and Tomlinson, who had orders to shoot the prisoners down if they attempted to escape.

Irquoi was quite easy about those within the cave.

They knew of only one other way out, and that was "no out at all," being the way by the river, where the rapid waters shut them out from exit.

Nobody thought of sleeping that night, but steps were taken to make themselves secure against any attack then or in the immediate future.

The position had been well chosen by the original squatters, for the only way in, save down by the hill sides, was the path by which Herbert and his party came.

It was true that by the same law there was only one way out, but with the prospect of an attacking party dwindling down to the finest point they were not at all uneasy on that score.

Hitherto Herbert had hesitated to ask Irquoi about his encounter with Nero, but now that his father was restored to him he entered into the subject, and learnt that the apparently desperate fight had hardly been a fight at all.

All the dog strove to do was to get Irquoi down and hold him on the ground. He was too noble a beast to worry a man, as a rule, and his instincts probably told him that in the main, Irquoi was not a real foe.

The savage escaped, as we know, by plunging into the river.

He dived and was carried a long way under water ; then he swam as Nero was borne out to sea, and was finally successful in reaching the shore.

But he saw no more of Nero.

And now a few words about the captivity of James Standish and Richard Warden.

Sprague and his friends had succeeded in creeping up to the huts, and casting some of the mysterious liquid made by Irquoi over them.

Overpowered by the poison they fell insensible and were carried away to the cave.

Once there they were imprisoned in an inner cave, the mouth of which was blocked and food passed through a small hole daily.

They were often assured that at a given time they would be set free, but did not place much faith in the promise.

So they worked away with their hands at the strong barricade, and by that slow process eventually got it down on the very night that Herbert entered the cave.

They were creeping along the dark way with the hopes of finding a road to liberty, when nine of their enemies, whom they did not even know by sight, discovered them.

They ran for their lives and came, as we have described, to where Herbert and his friends had succeeded in capturing some of the party.

It was superstition that saved their lives, as Sprague afterwards admitted.

They were averse to shedding white men's blood because it would bring them "ill-luck;" but they did not want anyone prowling around them.

They suspected that Herbert, his father, and Richard Warden had come there with the same object as themselves.

So they took measures to put an end to the quest as far as they were concerned, and the discovery that they had simply been wrecked, set Sprague off on one of his characteristic pieces of eloquence.

"It's a downright settler, that's what it is," he said; "we've been putting powder into our own fire and blown everything to Jericho. Dern that ere Irquoi! Why didn't we string him up, as we said we would, more than once?"

Irquoi, of course, had learnt to look upon all white men as his enemies, and that is why he had given assistance to his original foes.

He it was who removed the tools from the camp after having drugged Nero by the now familiar process; but he had no hand in capturing Herbert in the cave.

The adventurers did that bit of bamboozling, and the same superstition that saved James Standish's life, saved that of his son.

It was not at all owing to any really merciful considerations, and he owed them no thanks. They put him outside because they were running short of provisions.

And they placed him in a spot where he had a good chance on awakening of falling down and breaking his neck or drowning.

"That wouldn't have been murder on our part," they reasoned.

All these things came out in due time, but we

After a time of privation they sighted a trader outward bound.

put them on record here so that the reader may not be unduly hampered with too many mysteries capable of explanation.

All night long the party kept awake, but towards morning the prisoners slept.

They were an ungainly, awkward-looking lot, with faces most unpleasant to look upon. Brave in their way, but unscrupulous if they dare be to serve their own ends.

What was to be done with them in the cave? Should they be left there to starve?

That was not at all a British way of doing things, and as Irquoi said they could be got at and communicated with, an effort to do so was resolved upon.

And now we come to the mystery of the cave upon the hill where the provisions of our friends had been stored and lost.

Irquoi, as it proved, was, with Tualcamachi, responsible for that.

In the cave was a way into the great underground arteries of which the white men knew nothing.

At the bottom was a similar "door" to that which had been closed over the known entrance to the cave.

Irquoi would show it to Herbert gladly, and by it they would enter the greater cave ; and, from what he called "high perch," see a wonderful thing.

"Here—no see—no shoot at," he said.

"I am ready when you are," said Herbert. "It is time all this business was over."

James Standish would not part again with his son so he accompanied them, and the rest were left to guard the prisoners.

Tualcamachi remained behind also, looking gloomy and sad.

CHAPTER XX.

GOOD FORTUNE AT LAST—CAGED ENEMIES.

"G REAT eye — lose — NOW," said the king. "No more worship of star—no star to worship."

Only Irquoi understood what he meant, and he offered him a few words of consolation, which had no marked effect upon him.

Back through the path to the open country, and thence round to the spot where an attempt had been made to build a boat.

The wreck of their work was blown in a heap by the great storm into a hollow which, with the timber and stuff piled into it, bore a resemblance to what is known as a " dug out " among travellers.

As they drew near it, Herbert thought he heard a faint whining sound inside, and a hope of finding an old friend there flashed upon him.

It died out almost as soon as it came ; but it was to be fulfilled.

In the hollow among the *débris* lay poor Nero, thin as a rake, blear-eyed with exposure and suffering, and barely able to move.

" Oh ! Nero—Nero," said Herbert, " I am glad to see you, even as you are."

He was quite overcome, and put his arms about the neck of the dog, who feebly licked his cheek.

They had brought food for a day with them, but all thought of self vanished in a moment. They began at once to feed the starving beast.

Nero ate ravenously. He devoured all they had, and with the little strength it gave him was able to get upon his feet.

In a cramped way he turned his steps to the river, and on its being reached, cooled his hard, dry tongue with the limpid water.

It restored him amazingly, but he was still very weak, and could only just hobble behind them.

The dog could not tell his story, but it was easily guessed at.

He had succeeded in getting ashore, after being carried out to sea, in an exhausted condition, there to encounter the fury of the storm.

No doubt he had been sorely bruised and battered by it, but he managed to get back to the camp, which he found deserted, and in doggy despair crept into the storm-made "dug-out" to die.

But so far all was going well with our friends, and it really seemed as if the clouds of misfortune were at length dispersed.

With lighter hearts than they known for days, they followed Irquoi up to the hill to the sloping shaft-like cave.

Untroubled by fears they entered, comforted by the assurance of the savage that it "no much dark dere," and with cautious tread reached the bottom.

Then Irquoi put aside a sliding stone, not so big as the other, but leaving an opening wide enough for a man to walk through if he stooped a little.

"Go slow," he said. "It de home of de Great Star."

The three adventurers had not far to go.

Followed by Nero, who every now and then gave vent to a satisfied whine, they traversed a low passage, about twenty feet in length, and then emerged upon a small underground hall, dimly lighted by means of a variety of perforations in the roof.

It was a place well calculated to excite in the travellers the most unbounded astonishment.

In the first place it was perfectly clear that this place had been fashioned out of the rock by man.

It was almost a perfect dome, and round the centre of it ran a rude gallery—a ledge of almost five feet broad with a low parapet.

On to this the travellers emerged.

But the great wonder of the place was a metal star of about two feet in diameter, suspended from the roof.

It had a least a dozen points, and on each point gleamed a big diamond.

In the centre was one as big as all the others put together.

"De star—*our* star," said Irquoi, sadly. "Now you look, now you see. *It is yours.*"

"Why ours?" asked Herbert. "What right have we to it?"

"No good to Tualcamachi any more," said Irquoi, "so wise star-worshipper say—dat why Tualcamachi sad. But you have it—good ; oder white men have it—bad."

Irquoi was very earnest in his manner, and Herbert and his father thought that it would be foolish to ignore the chance of taking possession of such valuable jewels, the sale of which would give them the wealth they left home to find.

To obtain it they had left their native land poor in purse, but rich in all that makes true manhood.

Here was what they wanted thrust into their hands by a strange series of events, and why should they not avail themselves of it?

They asked Irquoi if he knew how the star became fixed there and the origin of its worship.

He told them, in his broken way, that Tualcama-chi and his ancestors had worshipped it so long ago that man could not count the time.

But this view of the facts might, as his listeners knew, have referred to no more than a century or so.

The reckoning power of savages is very limited, and small numbers are big things in their eyes.

It was pretty clear that Sprague and his friends had come hither in search of that star, having by some means obtained an inkling of its existence.

On this point Irquoi could not enlighten them.

"Dey come," he said, "look for it—make me much laugh—but no find."

Then came the question about getting down that star, and Irquoi put that question at rest by announcing that it could be dislodged from above by the removal of a few stones.

Then he showed them a narrow flight of steps leading down to the floor of this strange underground hall and left them.

"Soon come back," he said.

James Standish and Herbert stood aside, awaiting the fall of the star, which hung about twenty feet over their heads; but the minutes flew by, and it remained above with no sign of movement from Irquoi.

The light crept downward through a series of very minute crevices, but if anyone had passed over them the temporary shadow would be observable.

A suspicion of having been betrayed began to take possession of them.

What real love could Irquoi or his king bear the white man, and was it not natural that they should seek to destroy ALL who had invaded their land?

But though both thought it neither would give it utterance as yet, for which they were afterwards glad, for suddenly after a long delay down came the star with a rush, a stiff rope of some sort of wire coiling above it.

Overhead from an opening the light poured down, and the voice of Irquoi was heard.

"Him stick much, but he down now."

They looked up and saw his face grinning through the opening. Then with a nod of satisfaction he disappeared.

A few minutes more and he was back again, standing behind them, while they were examining the star.

The rope was of some sort of grassy fibre with gold wire interwoven with it, and the star itself was of solid gold.

The setting of the magnificent stones was a splendid piece of workmanship.

To carry the whole away as it was could not be done, so with their knives they turned up the points of the setting and carefully removed the precious stones.

There were thirteen in all—the supposed unlucky number; but the fortunate finders were not troubled about that matter—they were not superstitious.

Herbert Standish carefully placed the treasure in an inner pocket of the tunic he wore, and Irquoi, coiling the rope about the star, tossed it aside.

"Come by-bye for dat," he said.

"And how about our friends in the cave?" said James Standish.

"Not far," replied Irquoi, with a grin; "me hear dem."

That was more than his companions could do; but Irquoi was quite confident, and with that satisfied smile upon his face he walked to the side of the hall opposite to the place by which he had entered, and pulled out a big stone, which seemed to be part of the solid rock.

Several others fell out also—so that a pretty wide opening was shown—big enough for two persons to enter abreast.

"Soon find light," said Irquoi; "soon come—stop —say shoot—give up speak-fire to Irquoi."

Father and son grasped his meaning readily. From the gallery above they would have the command of the opening and shoot down anyone who might have the temerity to emerge.

The nine entombed men, if they came that way, would be called upon to give up their weapons ere they came forth—and what was to be done with the men themselves was an after consideration.

A sign to Irquoi was sufficient, and he took up a position by the side of the mouth of the cave. Herbert and his father hastened to the gallery above.

And then they waited for the men who had passed a long and weary night in that strange catacomb-like place.

Their lamps, none of the best, had all gone out, and they were groping about in the dark in despair, when a faint ray of light was observable ahead.

With a shout of joy they rushed towards it, and

presently, within a few yards of this opening to be suddenly checked in their movements by a loud, clear voice, crying—

"Stand! or you will be shot."

They pulled up, huddling together in affright, as any body of men might be excused for doing under such circumstances.

They knew nothing of the foe in front of them— could see nobody; but the voice certainly came from some one well under cover.

"Throw out your arms and weapons of every sort and yield yourselves, then no harm will come to you!"

"And suppose we don't do it?" asked one of the men.

"Then we shall fire upon you, and those who are left alive will be boxed up where you are. There will be no way of escape left for you."

But the men still hesitated, and were whispering together when James Standish gave them a final word.

"Do it at once—there will be no dallying in the matter. No harm is intended you—if you are sensible men."

They hesitated no longer, but tossed out the revolvers and bowie knives they carried, one of each to every man—eighteen in all.

At a signal from James Standish—who had not yet been seen by his foes—Irquoi quickly gathered up the weapons, the men in the passage cursing him soundly as he did so.

But for obvious reasons they did not think it prudent to carry out their desire to rush out upon him and belabour him to death.

When Irquoi had picked up all he hastened to

join the exultant pair above, and his swarthy face was positively shining with joy.

"Got all now," he said ; "do noting."

"Well, there are nine of them," said James Standish, "and what is to be done with them ?"

"Leave them here for the present," said Herbert. "I suppose we can block up the way here ?"

Irquoi said it could be done easily.

"Little flat stone outside," he said, "keep big stone shut."

"Come then," said James Standish, "and such words of comfort as we can give our friends here shall be delivered from above."

The whole thing had happened in a fortuitous manner bordering on the miraculous ; but lucky events like misfortunes seldom come singly.

The tide was now running wholly in the favour of our friends, and the wind of good luck may be considered to be blowing on the beam, about the best way for a ship to sail by.

Their retreat was easy, and they left the nine bewildered men in the cave in ignorance of the force to which they had surrendered, until they appeared above.

"In a little time," said James Standish, peering down from the hole in the roof made by the removal of the star, "and I will send your comrades to you."

"Are you alone ?" asked one of the men, savagely.

"No," replied James Standish, "I have my son with me, and Irquoi."

"No more ?"

"That is all."

Then the nine men began to curse and rage, and

they ramped round the hall like caged wild beasts, while the father and son listened to Irquoi's explanation of how the star had been fixed.

The rope had been fastened to a stout bar of gold embedded in the earth, and the spot carefully covered up with stones. The bar of gold was lying on the ground, and that they could take away with them.

" I think we will leave them the rest," said Herbert, with a smile ; " it is only fair that after having fished so long that they should have the shell of the oyster."

" Hullo ! there, you two," roared one of the men " is there any way out here ?"

" Yes," replied Herbert, "through the hole in the root. Good-day !"

CHAPTER XXI.

DEATH OF TUALCAMACHI.

OTH father and son on returning to the camp found a sad and solemn scene awaiting them.

Tualcamachi, the old savage king was lying at the point of death.

It was so sudden that to Herbert the tidings was a shock, and he hastened to the old man's side to see if anything could be done for him.

But it was evident that the end was near.

He lay upon a grassy slope, with one of the sailor's jackets rolled up under his head.

All that could be done for him had been done, but he had partaken of neither drink nor food, having persistently refused both.

He looked up at Herbert with a faint smile on his face.

"Very old—time to go—de star GONE. It better. No bring good to *my* people."

Then Irquoi drew up to him, and knelt down by his side.

"Forgive Irquoi," he said.

"Good Irquoi," murmured the old man, and he laid a hand upon his head as if blessing him.

Not another word escaped him. A little later on he closed his eyes and peacefully went into the sleep from which there is no awakening in this world.

By what strange law of nature this old man suddenly succumbed, we know not, but it is no great novelty in savage life.

There is a tribe in one of the Pacific islands to whom sickness is unknown ; but on a certain day one of them will announce his approaching death in a calm manner, just as if he were going out for a walk.

Forthwith he retires to his hovel, and in a few hours is no more.

They make up their minds to die, and thus it must have been with Tualcamachi.

He had lived to see his tribe scattered, and all his kingly glory, such as it was, depart from him, so he welcomed death.

Irquoi's grief was for a brief space of time very violent ; but he soon became ca'mer, and set about preparing for the interment of his king.

He refused all assistance, saying that no man must know where the body of Tualcamachi would be laid, and alone he bore it away.

During his absence Herbert had an interview with Sprague, who seemed to be a bit of a philosopher in his way, and accepted his position calmly.

Not a word was said to him about the discovery and appropriation of the Star.

He was simply questioned as to the object he and his friends had in coming there.

He frankly told his story.

They came there to discover a treasure which Sprague's grandfather, an old American sailor, had told them would be found in the caves.

He gave them a full description of the spot on the west coast of Africa where it could be found, and told them exactly the class of natives they would have to deal with.

He also located the caves ; but the actual spot where this treasure could be found he did not know, as he had only heard of it from an old shipmate who talked in his cups and declined to give full particulars.

"And on the strength of that story you came here ?" said Herbert.

"Yes, we are a speculative people," replied Sprague, "and having had a streak of luck at the silver mines we clubbed together and fitted out a fair-sized yacht. Most of my pards are sailors, and they run the vessel over. Finding the country and people as described we went on with the business."

'But you did not find the treasure?" said Herbert.

"No ; hang it ! Although we've dug and dug our very hearts out. We thought you'd got hold of the yarn and come on the same quest—more blamed fools we.   If we'd let you alone we might ha' been going on all right now."

"Well, you can go on again," said Herbert, coolly, "for we are going to borrow your yacht to get home with.   You've acted rather rough to us, so you cannot expect much compunction in this matter on our part."

"I s'pose not," replied Sprague ; "but, hang it all, you won't leave us to frizzle here for ever, will you ?"

"No," returned Herbert ; "we will try to make arrangements for your rescue ; but if we consider ourselves first in this matter you have only to thank yourselves "

It was late in the afternoon when Irquoi came back.   Meanwhile, Herbert had sent some food and water to the prisoners in the cave by Sam Gorgon and Tomlinson, who had instructions to lower it through the hole in the ceiling of the cave.

It was a task that suited both admirably.

" Jest like the way them Romans I've read of fed their wild beasts," said Sam, "and they snarled much the same way — not at the vittles, but at us."

Tomlinson asked them what they were doing down there, and why they didn't go out for a walk in the fresh air, and the language they used to him was awful.

In a consultation between Herbert, his father, and the two Trevelyns, it was decided to go the yacht at once, taking their three captives with them.

Irquoi knew where it was, and he was their guide.

An hour after the sun had gone down the light

of the young moon revealed it to them lying in a snug retreat—a small natural harbour.

It was a yacht of about one hundred tons, and they could get aboard of her by means of a boat upon the shore.

She was well furnished in everything, Sprague told them, but provisions, of which there was but a small store.

But all our friends were sick of the country in which they had spent such an exciting time ; and stores or no stores they decided to get away.

"But what about our own ?" exclaimed David Trevelyn—"the lot lost in the cave ?"

Irquoi had, as we have stated, removed them, and he said they were all in a recess in the gallery. He had forgotten them.

So had Herbert in the excitement of the discovery of the Diamond Star and the subsequent events.

It was now too late to think of returning for them.

"Let us get away with what we have," said James Standish. "Take a good supply of water, and risk the rest."

"And so say all of us," said Ginger.

And it was carried *nem. con.*

Then the plans they had devised were put into operation.

First, one of the prisoners was released, and told to march straight away on pain of being shot.

He lost no time in obeying this injunction.

Then a second one was despatched, and, finally, Sprague's arms were loosened.

To him was imparted the secret of the place of confinement of his nine friends, also about the hiding-place of the stores.

"Which may be useful to you," said James Standish, "as there is a prospect of your prolonging your stay here for some considerable time."

"I'd like to ask a question of you afore I go," said Sprague, looking round at the men ready to carry out their threat to shoot if he attempted an attack upon one of them.

"Well, what is it?" asked Herbert.

"You've got the mopusses," said Sprague, "but I don't see it about you. None of you look bulky."

"It is only a few diamonds," said James Standish, "value, as I judge, about two hundred thousand pounds."

"Snakes!" exclaimed Sprague. "Well, when my pards know it I reckon they will skip around."

He put his hands into his pockets and went off with his head down, a very fair specimen of a man overwhelmed by defeat.

"Irquoi," said Herbert, to the savage, "you will go with us?"

"All place," replied Irquoi, with one of his sweeping, graceful bows."

So they all got into the boat, and pulled to the yacht, which lay about a quarter of a mile off shore, and were soon on board.

There was no wind—there seldom was at night in that latitude—so they hauled up the boat, and took it in turns to watch for the morning.

The only way the men they had left ashore could get aboard was by swimming, and they were hardly likely to attempt that.

Nero was with the party, of course, and when he had been assisted up to the deck he lay down and gave a contented sigh, as much as to say—

Finally Sprague's arms were loosened.

"All troubles are at an end. Peace and rest at last."

In the morning a breeze sprung up and Ginger and the men set to work to fix the sails. While they were thus engaged Sam Gorgon, who was leaning over the side, uttered a shout.

"Here they are," he said; "all of them!"

Yes, there they were on the shore; twelve defeated and almost maddened men.

They ran up and down like wild dogs, absolutely *barking* in their rage, and it was ludicrous to see them pick up stones and hurl them at the yacht, which was far and away out of the reach of such missiles.

"Richard Warden," said James Standish, "I reckon this is about as sweet a revenge as we could have. It is better than killing them. Even poor Carrol, if he could know of it, would consider himself avenged."

Richard Warden smiled.

"I am quite satisfied," he said.

An hour after the little yacht with its party was out of the harbour, and six miles or so from the scene of so many strange adventures.

That night James Standish made a proposition to his fellow wanderers, which was gladly and gratefully accepted.

If ever they reached a civilised land the diamonds were to be sold.

Half of the proceeds to go to the Standishes, and the rest to be divided among their comrades.

"More than fair," said Richard Warden. "There is no reason in equity why you do not keep the whole."

"No more travelling for me," said Sam Gorgon,

"not even as a commercial in the old country. I shall open a business somewhere, get hold of a useful wife, one who has been manageress of some millinery department in a big house, and settle down."

"Well, let us hope," said David Trevelyn, "that we all do something sensible with our money—when we get it."

CHAPTER XXII.

THE DROP SCENE.

FIVE months afterwards the party landed at Liverpool.

After a time of privation at sea in their little yacht they fell in with a trader outward bound to New York, and having no money to pay for provisions, wisely abandoned the little craft, and what eventually became of it was never known.

They were taken to New York, where James Standish sold one of the smallest diamonds for ten thousand pounds.

He had to explain that he had found it in that far-off land before the sale could be completed, and as nobody had lost such a thing and interference with him was impossible he was paid the money.

The jewel was purchased by a Yankee millionaire as a birthday present for his wife.

The captain of the vessel which picked them up was handsomely rewarded, and the crew not forgotten, then passages home for the whole party were taken.

They arrived, as we have said, at Liverpool, and from thence proceeded to London, where James Standish put himself in communication with one of the most noted bankers with whom at one time he had an account, and through him the diamonds were disposed of.

Only the richest could buy them, and the large one was purchased for an emperor as one of the rarest jewels in the world.

The united sales, when all expenses and commissions were paid, realised two hundred and ten thousand pounds.

It was so quietly carried out that the world heard little of it, and Herbert and his father went into Berkshire to settle in a quiet country home.

Originally James Standish had been a fairly rich man, but was robbed of all by a friend, who held a high position as a lawyer whom he trusted.

Now all that was forgotten and forgiven, and once more he was the country gentleman.

Richard Warden lived near them, and settled down as the bachelor of the village, but Herbert ere long married one of the sweetest girls in Berkshire, which, of course, was somebody very sweet indeed.

The two Trevelyns went abroad with their money and started mining on a big scale. They have been very successful.

Sam Gorgon has now a drapery and general establishment of such a vast extent that it is quite a hard task to saunter all over it. He has become both rich and fat, but he is a kind employer and a good fellow all round.

As for Ginger and the seamen, they, acting on ames Standish's advice, bought an annuity with two-thirds of their money and then, sailor-like, went on the "spree" with the rest.

But their spreeing was mainly good fellowship,

and many a poorer Jack-tar had reason to bless them for their generosity.

Down Wapping way they made things lively for a week or so, and then started on a round, visiting a number of seaports, and spending freely among their brother tars, until the surplus was exhausted.

Then, like sensible men, they decided to settle down.

Ginger and Tomlinson are married and live by the sea on the East Coast, where they can get a good blow all the year round.

Starbutt and Spifley are somewhat erratic in their movements, living here and there, but they enjoy life, and they don't squander health with dissipation.

They have all had a black star tattooed on their arms in commemoration of their adventures.

Irquoi is an attendant or servant in Herbert's house, but he has no specified duties.

In civilised attire he is not quite so picturesque a being as he used to be; but he is a lasting object of interest to the village, where his strength and agility are themes of much juvenile and adult admiration.

Herbert had been married about a year when he read in a daily paper of twelve men who had been rescued from a lone place on the African coast and brought to England.

They said they were Americans, and according to their account had been some time on the coast, and had almost degenerated into a wild state.

A year afterwards a wild beast show came down to Berkshire, and Herbert, with others, went to it.

A real wild man was advertised as being exhibited, and during the afternoon he was brought out of a caravan and placed upon a platform for the audience to see.

He was changed, but Herbert instantly recognised him.

It was Sprague.

He had grown a vast quantity of hair about his head and face, and looked wild enough for a show; but he did not seem unhappy.

Herbert was not recognised by him, and, of course, he did not wish to make himself known; so he went quietly home, and Sprague, on the morrow, journeyed on for exhibition elsewhere.

"Life is a strange thing and there are many sides to it," and the career of those who have figured in this story is a proof of it.

One word as a finale about that star on Tomlinson's breast. It is there still, and the secret of its manufacture is locked up in Irquoi's heart.

"No make here," he says, "no stuff for it. Me neber tell—no good to anyone."

And that is about the true state of the case—"The Brand of the Black Star" cannot be put upon any of us here.

THE END.

BUZFUZ, the champion quoit-player, of High-street, Peckham, buys some rockets to illuminate his birthday—or rather birtheve. Naughty, idle boy comes along with a vesuvian, and Satan finds a job for him.

Buzfuz keeps his birthday among the planets. Last heard of waltzing round Venus.

THE "BEST FOR BOYS" LIBRARY
(CHING CHING'S OWN).

Declared by Untold Thousands of Readers to be the most entertaining and mirth-provoking books ever written for Boys.

COMPLETE VOLUMES, PRICE 3d. each.

THE WILD ADVENTURES OF EDDARD AND JAM JOSSER ABROAD.

THE SLAPCRASH BOYS. A LIVELY SCHOOL STORY.

THE WILD ADVENTURES OF EDDARD AND JAM JOSSER AT HOME.

THE BRAND OF THE BLACK STAR.

VALIANT ROY; OR, THE PIRATES' SCOURGE.

COMPLETE VOLUMES, PRICE 6d. each.

JACK OF THE GOLDEN BELT; OR, STIRRING ADVENTURES IN THE GREAT SWAMPS OF CUBA.

YOUNG CHING AT SCHOOL; OR, HIGH OLD TIMES FOR THE SLAPCRASHERS.

OUR BOYS ABROAD; OR, THE BLACK BANDITS OF THE RHINE.

THE VEILED CAPTAIN; OR, THE HERO OF EAGLE CRAIG.

GALLANT HAL; OR, THE CRUISE OF THE SILVER STAR.

DICK STORNAWAY; OR, A HERO IN SPITE OF HIS FOES.

CHING CHING AND HIS CHUMS; A MOST MIRTHFUL, MOVING, AND MYSTERIOUS STORY.

DARING CHING CHING. A WONDROUS TALE.

COMPLETE VOLUMES, PRICE 1s. each.

TOM TARTAR AT SCHOOL. VOLS. I. AND II.

HANDSOME HARRY OF THE FIGHTING BELVEDERE. VOLS. I. AND II.

YOUNG CHING CHING. VOLS. I. AND II.

CHEERFUL CHING CHING.

WONDERFUL CHING CHING.

COMPLETE VOLUMES, PRICE 2s. each.

HANDSOME HARRY OF THE FIGHTING BELVEDERE.

TOM TARTAR AT SCHOOL; OR, TRUE FRIEND AND NOBLE FOE.

YOUNG CHING CHING. ANOTHER WONDROUS TALE.

TRAMP: "Here you are, sir; there's your clothes, and thank your stars an honest young man came along to give 'em to you. Some low people would have stolen 'em."

HIS LAST MISTAKE.

He was a warrior of intemperate habits, and he had often seen them at home, and found them nought but visions of a distempered mind. But when he was stationed in the tropics, on seeing a real one he hailed it as an old friend.

[They buried him before sundown, where the perfumes from the Spice Islands were wafted over his grave. Poor fellow—he wanted them badly!]

THE ONE GREAT PERIL OF THEIR HONEYMOON.

"OH! what is it, James; a bounding bison or a wild buffaler? Farewell! One more kiss before we die together!"

[They kissed; but they did not die after all. The furious beast mercifully spared them, and, in ddition, gave them some milk for tea.]

SILLY LITTLE JIMMY : "I can hear something coming."
WICKED TOMMY (his treacherous friend) : "You will feel it in a minute."
[Which Jimmy did.]

Printed by

Sully and Ford,

Plough Court,

Fetter Lane,

London.

www.ingramcontent.com/pod-product-compliance
Lightning Source LLC
Chambersburg PA
CBHW080830250626
47160CB00008B/2889